国家出版基金项目
NATIONAL PUBLICATION FOUNDATION

Planned by Zhuang Zhixiang   Edited by Pan Wenguo

READINGS OF CHINESE CULTURE SERIES

POETRY IV

An Anthology of the Tang Dynasty Poetry

Translated by Sun Dayu

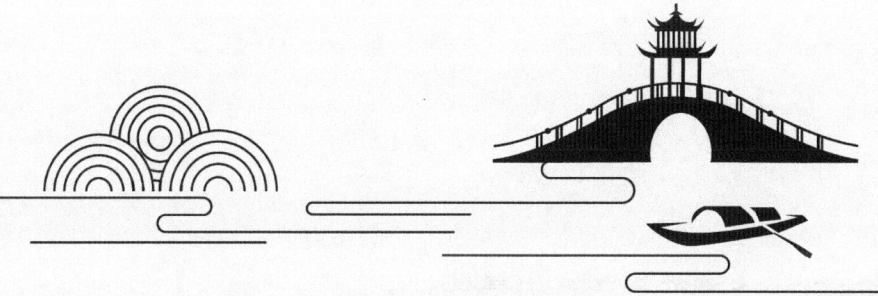

中国经典文化走向世界丛书

诗歌卷 四

庄智象◎总策划   潘文国◎总主编

孙大雨◎译

上海外语教育出版社
SHANGHAI FOREIGN LANGUAGE EDUCATION PRESS
www.sflep.com

图书在版编目（CIP）数据

中国经典文化走向世界丛书. 诗歌卷. 四 / 孙大雨
译. – 上海：上海外语教育出版社, 2018 (2024重印)
ISBN 978-7-5446-5551-4

Ⅰ. ①中… Ⅱ. ①孙… Ⅲ. ①中国文学－综合
作品集－ 英文 ②诗集－中国—英文 Ⅳ. ①I211

中国版本图书馆CIP数据核字（2018）第207211号

出版发行：**上海外语教育出版社**
　　　　　（上海外国语大学内）　邮编：200083
电　　话：021-65425300 （总机）
电子邮箱：bookinfo@sflep.com.cn
网　　址：http://www.sflep.com
责任编辑：梁瀚杰

印　　刷：苏州市古得堡数码印刷有限公司
开　　本：635×965　1/16　印张 11　字数174千字
版　　次：2018 年 11月第 1 版　2024 年 3月第 2 次印刷

书　　号：ISBN 978-7-5446-5551-4 / I
定　　价：35.00 元
　　　　本版图书如有印装质量问题, 可向本社调换
　　　　质量服务热线：4008-213-263

"Cherish one's own beauty, respect other's beauty, and when both beauties are respected and cherished, the world will become one", said Fei Xiaotong, a famous Chinese sociologist at a celebration party in honor of his eightieth birthday about thirty years ago. In a time of growing interest in intercultural communication today, these words sound especially wise and far-sighted. Translation, as one of the most important means for cultural communication, is usually done into one's mother tongue from other languages by native translators. This largely guarantees the quality of translated text, so far as the linguistic readability is concerned. However, this method implies a one-sidedness in correspondence, as only the translator's "respect for other's beauty" is concerned, regardless, though not completely, of how the local people look upon and cherish their own beauty. It should be compensated by translations on the other way, that is, works selected, interpreted, and translated by the local people themselves into languages other than their own. This approach may go directly against the prevalent views in modern translation theories but, in my opinion, is worthy of practicing. It is perhaps an even more effective way to bring about successful communication in cultures, and the beauties of the world can really be shared by the world's people. It is with such understanding that the Shanghai Foreign Language Education Press is organizing a new series of books, entitled *Readings of Chinese Culture*, to introduce Chinese culture, past and present, to the world, with works selected and translated by the Chinese scholars and translators.

The series will cover a wide range of writings including but not restricted to works of different literary genres. For the first batch, we are glad to provide three books of essays and one book of short stories, all written by authors of the 20th century. They will be continued by a batch of serious academic writings on premodern Chinese classics in philosophy, literature, and historiography, written by influential scholars of our time.

Later, we will offer more books on classical Chinese drama, classical Chinese poetry, etc.

Some of the books in the series have been published before, but they have been revised and rearranged for the new purpose to meet the current needs of broader readers. We are looking forward to hearing comments and suggestions on the series for future improvement.

Pan Wenguo

CONTENTS

An Anthology of the Tang Dynasty Poetry

Song on Ascending the Youzhou Terrace

◎ *Chen Zi'ang*[1]

Descrying nor the ancients of long yore,
Nor those that are to come in the future far,
I muse on the eternity of heaven and earth,
And, all alone, grieve mutely with tears for my lorn star.

Random Lines on Home-Coming

◎ *He Zhizhang*[2]

Parting from home a stripling still
And coming back old already,
I keep my local speech tone unchanged,
With temple locks grizzled and scanty.
Village boys knowing me not at sight
As a wayfaring trekker,
Laughingly ask wherefrom doth hail
The elderly stranger.

[1] Chen Zi'ang (661 – 702), courtesy name Boyu, a reformist poet of the early period of the Tang Dynasty.
[2] He Zhizhang (circa 659 – 744), courtesy name Jizhen, a famous poet and calligrapher.

Feelings on My State

◎ *Zhang Jiuling*[1]

(I)

The eupatory leaves grow lush in spring;
The osmanthus sprigs in autumn bloom pure and sweet.
Luxuriant doth wax their rest of life,
To make both seasons festive occasions meet.
Who knoweth the forest-dweller smelling the breeze
Diffused with fragrant odours loveth them with delight?
The plants bear natural qualities of their own;
Why need the Beauteous One pluck them himself to bedight?

(II)

To the south of the River the cinnabar orange doth thrive;
In the winter it still is in shrubbery of virgin green.
'Tis not only the earth cherishing its roots is mild and gentle,
But the vigour to stand severe cold in the plant lieth supreme.
The mature radiant fruit is fit to be offered to fair guests,
Had there been not hindrances cumbrous and rampant to obstruct.[2]
One's destiny could only be put up with sufferance dumb;
The dubious rule of vicissitudes cannot be traced before.
It is said timely planting of peach and plum trees giveth shade;
How is this goodly shrub not rewarded with both shade and fruit?

---

① Zhang Jiuling (678 – 740), courtesy name Zishou, a prominent poet of the Tang Dynasty. He served as the prime minister during the reign of Emperor Xuanzong.
② This and the following two lines allude to his fine statesmanship being put to naught by the trust of Emperor Xuanzong laid on his adversary as premier, the vicious Li Linfu (李林甫).

Ascending the Stork Tower

◎ *Wang Zhihuan*[1]

Behind the mounts daylight doth glow and fail,
The Luteous River to the sea doth flow.
The view of a thousand *li* to command,
Up a storey higher thou shouldst now go.

Liang County Song[(1)]

◎ *Wang Zhihuan*

The Luteous River glares heavenwards to the white clouds,
And a lorn pile lies by a mount a hundred furlongs high.
Why need the Qiang flute plain in a song of *Plucking Willows*?
Spring breezes would not be wafted out of the Jade Gate Pass.

Spring Dawn

◎ *Meng Haoran*[2]

Feeling not when cometh th' peep of spring dawn,
Everywhere birds' songs I hear in my slumber.
Through the sounds of wind and rain all th' night long,
Know I not how many th' flowers fall in number.

---

[1] Wang Zhihuan (688 – 742), courtesy name Jiling, an important "High Tang" poet. Only six of his poems are known to us now, but all are very successful.
[2] Meng Haoran (689 – 740), the first important landscape poet of the Tang Dynasty. His poems enjoyed a high reputation both in his lifetime and posthumously.

3

A Song on Listening to An Wanshan Playing the *Bi-Li* Pipe[2]

◎ *Li Qi*[1]

Cutting bamboo from the South Mount, a *bi-li* pipe is made by;
Qiuci the Hu state is where its bizarre music cometh from.
Growing current in the Celestial Empire, it turneth weird;
My Hu friend from Liangzhou doth upon it for me perform.
Neighbours of mine listening to it cannot but utter sighs,
Faraway wanderers thinking of home become tearful all.
People at large like to hear it without sounding its tune motif,
Hurricane wild cometh and goeth freely in its swift call.
Mulberry withered and cypress old seemeth its ringing sound;
A chirping phoenix with nine small chicks nestling against her down;
A dragon groaning or a tiger roaring loud[3] all at once,
And soon springs bubble forth, gusts of wind are rising and blow
    along,
All of a sudden then burst out the drum beats in a hail storm[4],
Dull dun clouds cover the sky to make daylight darken with gloom.
The pipe tune turneth its note to *Spring Breeze Breathing on the*
    Willows[5]:
Imperial garden flowers are all blazing in full bloom.
On New Year's Eve, in a high hall is lighted a host of candles;
One beaker of deep-delved wine with one *bi-li* pipe song to boom.

---

① Li Qi (circa 690 – circa 751), a "High Tang" poet well-known for his works on the frontier life.

Bidding Adieu to a Friend[1]

◎ *Wang Wei*[2]

As thou alight from thy horse,
I greet thee with a stoup of wine,
And ask thee whither thou wouldst tend.
Thy answer thou givest disheartened
Saying thou wouldst go to retire
As a recluse by the South Mount.
Go but thither without a query;
White clouds are there at all times.

---

[1] These lines were written by the poet to his friend Meng Haoran (孟浩然), also a friend of Li Bai (李白), and South Mount was the South Xian Mountain (南岘山) of Xiangyang (襄阳), now in Hubei Province (湖北).

[2] Wang Wei (circa 701 – 761), courtesy name Mojie, a poet, musician, and painter of the Tang Dynasty. He was one of the most famous men of arts and letters of his time. In his later years, Wang Wei turned to Buddhism and his poems reflected his focus on Zen practice; therefore, he was posthumously referred to as the "Poet Buddha".

Blue Runnel

◎ *Wang Wei*

In boating to the Yellow Flower Stream,
One should go coursing on the Blue Runnel down.
To cover the distance short of a hundred *li*,
The route windth round some ten thousand along.
The water roareth among a chaos of rocks,
The hills lie quiet beneath the thick pine trees.
Afloat on the waves are trapas and nymphaeas,
Reflected clearly are clumps of rushes and sedges.
Mine heart hath long been used to peace and calm;[1]
How this limpid stream is tranquil and pleasing!
I wish to remain here on this massive rock,
To spend my placid days in peace and angling.

Luanjia Rapids

◎ *Wang Wei*

Amidst the spattering showers autumnal,
The dashing rapids on the rocky band froth.
The leaping breakers splash 'gainst one another,
As an immaculate egret timidly steps forth.

---

[1] This and the line following indicate the harmony of the poet's state of mind as a recluse with the natural surroundings.

Bamboo Grove Cabin

◎ *Wang Wei*

Sitting alone in the thickset bamboo grove,
I plucked the heptachord to halloo and croon.
The thicket hidden being withdrawn from men,
I was shone on by the full luminous moon.

Bird-Chirping Hollow

◎ *Wang Wei*

The light beams of the moon on the earth softly rain,
The night is quiet, the spring mount empty,
The moon's uprise the birds doth frighten
To cry now and then in the springtide hollow.

Lines

◎ *Wang Wei*

Hailing from our good old homeland,
Thou ought to have tidings therefrom.
'Fore the caved windows thou passed that day,
Had the plum tree burst into blossom?

Smallholders' Homes by the Wei Stream

◎ *Wang Wei*

When slanting sunbeams shine on the village scene,
To the lanes retreated return all cattle and sheep.
Some rustics aged expecting the shepherd boys
Are waiting with their staffs at the brushwood doors.
He-pheasants clang and wheat stalks come to ear,
The mulberry leaves grow scant as silkworms sleep.
Farm hands now come up with their hoes on shoulders,
Seeing one another, fall they to talk with cheer.
In the air of all such leisurely good humour,
I yearn for a quiet hermit's life free and dear.

Remembering My Brothers East of the Mountain on the Ninth Day of the Ninth Moon

◎ *Wang Wei*

Being a stranger all alone
In a strange land far away,
I think of my parents all the more
On a fair festival day.
I know full well my brothers all
Would climb up the heights of a mount!
Inserting cornus shoots in their hair,
They'd all miss one in their count.

Bidding Adieu to Yuan Junior in His Mission to Anxi
(Song of the Town of Wei)

◎ *Wang Wei*

The fall of morning drops in this Town of Wei
Its dust light doth moisten,
Tenderly green are the new willow sprouts
Of this spring-adorned tavern.
I pray thee to quench once more full to the brim
This farewell cup of wine,
For after thy departure from this western-most pass,
Thou will have no old friend of thine.

Far Departed

◎ *Li Bai*[1]

Far departed, in days of distant yore,
There were the sisters Ehuang and Nüying[6],
From their common dear lord Zhonghua,
South of the wide expanse of Lake Dongting
At the limpid Xiang Stream's water margin.
Sad like huge waves surging
Bottomlessly in deep sea,
Who could say this life-forsaking
Severance is not heart-wringing?
Drearily shineth the sun, with
Murky clouds enshrouding;
Hear, oh hear! the chimpanzees are screeching
Smoke, and lo! the spirits weird are squirting
Raindrops fine and mistily thick.
What availeth though I speak of it?[7]
I do fear Divine Heaven cast not His splendour
On my sworn allegiance of fealty:[8]
Thunder-claps would crash down roaring
Through the masses of racks momently;
E'en Yao[9] and Shun would be dethroned to give place
To Yu. Sovereigns would lose their inferiors,
Dragons turn to finny soles, and power
Would be relegated to followers
As rats metamorphose into tigers.[10]

---

① Li Bai (701 – 762), courtesy name Taibai and style name Qinglian, one of the most acclaimed poets throughout Chinese history. Li Bai took the traditional poetic forms to new heights, and his works marked the "Golden Age of Chinese Poetry".

Sometimes people would quoth Yao was imprisoned in his time
And Shun died a lorn death in the wild;
On the Nine-peaked Dubious,
All tops alike and continuous,
Where doth lie the tomb lone
Of the duo-pupiled one?[11]
The bereaved princesses wept to mourn
In the green clouds of bamboo groves,
Waiting sore, while vanishing in the winds and
Looking far towards high mounts of Cangwu broad plain;
Unless the high Cangwu Mounts topple down all,
Their tear stains would keep fast on the verdant poles tall.[12]

Difficult Is the Way to Shu — A Pindaric Ode
(The Poem in Triple-Syllabic Measures)

◎ *Li Bai*

Yi-Xu-Xi!

How dangerously high and steep, the way to Shu
Is more difficult than ascending the blue sky!
Cancong and Yufu[(13)], it is mysteriously unknown how
They began to found their remotely ancient state.
Since then for forty-eight millennia
It had been separated from the Qin terrain.
In the west, it connecteth Noble White Alp[(14)] with a bird's
Flight route, and joineth with the topmost peak of Emei.
The earth yawned, the mountain crumbled, the five giants[(15)] died;
And then heavenward steps and rock-hewn flights of stairs are thus
    conjoined.
Up above there is the highest clift for Xihe[(16)]
To drive and turn his six dragons of the Sun-chariot round,
And down below there are the clashing currents of the whirling
    stream.
Yellow storks[(17)] could not fly over that and gibbons and hapales
Would be troubled by trying to climb up over it.
The Blue Sod Alps[(18)] twist and turn in winding about;
They twine round nine times to form peaks and pinnacles while
    whirling forth.
They pierce into the sky; on them you could touch the brilliant stars
While holding your breath and pressing a palm against your breast for
    heaving sighs.
Let me ask you when you would turn back from journeying westwards:

The fearful way and the sheer precipitous clifts are impassable and insurmountable.

You would only see sad birds crying on old trees;

The males followed by their females round the forests.

You would hear the cuckoos wailing at the moon, gasping out their griefs on bare mountain crests;

The way to Shu[19] is more difficult than ascending the azure sky;

The sad cries of the cuckoos[20] would make their hearers hasten to become old.

The chain of sharp peaks and pinnacles leaves the sky not a foot;

Withered pines hang beside the precipitous crags.

Flying rapids and dashing cataracts vie in their roarings;

The clashing of water against the rocks reverberates thunderbolts in ten thousands of hollows.

Such are the dangers, alas! why do you distant travellers come hither!

The Sword Steeple[21] towereth high up over dizzy flights of steps:

Let one valiant man block the pass, and ten thousand others cannot go through.

If the keeper is not an imperial kin, he might turn out to be a wolf or a hyena.

At morn, beware of tigers fierce; at dusk look out for gigantic serpents!

They would grind their teeth and swallow blood, and butcher people like mowing down hemp.

Although the city of officials robed in gold-threaded brocade is a city pleasurable,

It is better to forgo it for your own homes.

The way to Shu is more difficult than ascending the blue sky;

One turning to look westward could but heave long sighs.

Difficult Is the Way to Shu — A Pindaric Ode
(The Prose Version)

◎ *Li Bai*

Ah-hah ho! How dangerously high and steep, the way to Shu is more difficult than ascending the azure sky! Cancong and Yufu, it is mysteriously unknown how they began to found their state. Since then for forty-eight thousand years, it had been separated from the Qin terrain. In the west, it connecteth Noble White Alp with but a bird's flight route, and is joineth with the topmost peak of Emei. The earth yawned, the mountain crumbled, the five giants died; and then heavenward steps and rock-hewn flights of stairs are conjoined. Up above there is the highest clift for Xihe to drive and turn his six dragons of the Sun-chariot around, and down below there are the clashing currents of the whirling stream. Yellow storks could not fly over that and gibbons and hapales would be worried by trying to climb up it. The Blue Sod Alps twist and turn in winding about; they twine round nine times to form peaks and pinnacles while whirling forward. They pierce into the sky; on them you could touch the bright stars while holding your breath and pressing a palm against your breast and heaving sighs. Let me ask you when you would turn back from journeying westwards: the fearful way and the precipitous clifts are impassable and insurmountable. You could only see sad birds crying on the old trees; the male ones followed by their females round the forests. You would hear the cuckoos wailing at the moon, gasping out their griefs on bare mountain crests; the way to Shu is more difficult than ascending the blue sky; the sad cries of the cuckoos would make their hearers hasten to become old. The chain of sharp peaks and pinnacles leaveth the sky not a foot; withered pines hang beside the precipitous crags. Flying rapids and dashing cataracts vie in their roarings; the clashing of water against the rocks produceth thunderbolts in ten thousand hollows. Such are the dangers, alas! Why do you distant travellers come hither! The Sword Steeple towereth aloft: Let one valiant man block the pass, and ten thousand others could not go through it. If the keeper is not an imperial kin, he might turn to be a wolf or a hyena. At morn, beware of tigers fierce; at dusk, look out for giant serpents! They would grind their teeth and swallow blood, and butcher people like mowing down hemp. Although the city of officials robed in gold-threaded brocade is a city of pleasure, it is better to give it up for home. The way to Shu is more difficult than ascending the blue sky; one turning to look westward could but heave long sighs.

Crows Croaking at Dusk[22]

◎ *Li Bai*

By the town bulwalk, 'neath the sandy clouds,
The crows are setting down for the night.
Returning to nests and croaking one and all,
On branches of trees they come to alight.
To weave by hand her taffeta piece,[23]
The Qin Stream young dame plieth her loom
While speaking alone by herself at the window screen
Of smoky blue, of her drear doom.
She pauseth her shuttle to pine on her far-off lord;
All alone in her room, raineth tears in accord.

A Tune of Crows Roosting 'fore the Eve

◎ *Li Bai*

When crows for nests are roosting 'fore the eve
On Gusu Mount beside the Gusu Terrace[24],
The Wu state[25] king's enamoured belle Xishi
Is the carousal's darling of the Palace.
Before the Wu-toned songs and Chu-mode steps
Are sung and danced to the end with joy and fun,
The verdant mount above the east horizon
Is about to mouth some half a piece of the sun.
The silver arrow telleth the golden case
Of clepsydra hath dript its water enow[26];
Arise, see how the autumnal moon's sinking low
On the eastward flushing waves of the river flow;
The eastern sky is rising high, alas O!

Carouse, Please

◎ *Li Bai*

Seest thou not
the waters of the Luteous River rush down from the sky,
And roll off to the sea forevermore not to come back?
Seest thou not
White locks are wailed at before bright mirrors in halls high,
For turning at dusk into snowflakes from their morning's jet black?
Seize the moments of content in life and make full mirth of them;
Let not your golden beakers stay empty to glint at the moon.
Heaven hath endowed me with talents certes for good use;
A thousand pieces of gold being scattered'll come back soon.
Let mutton and beef be broiled for making merry;
We should drain three hundred bumpers at one carouse.
My friends sire Cen and good Danqiu, pause not in drinking,
Let me sing a ditty for you, let me your kind ears arouse.
Banquets with bell-strikings and drum-beats are not by me prized,
But I wish to drink deep always, ne'er sadly sober remain.
Since olden times, saints and sages have all been solitary,
While drinkers throughout the ages their renown do retain.
When King Chenzhi of literary fame feasted at Pingle
Ten thousand coins were spent on each dipper of rare old vintage.
Why doth our taverner say there is any lack of cash?
We should not lack means to get wine your mind to assuage.
My mottled steed and the fur-lined robe of a thousand crowns,
Let my boy lead and fetch out to barter for drinks divine,
In order to banish with ye both our griefs eternal trine.

The Lay of the Sun Arising and Sinking

◎ *Li Bai*

The sun ariseth from the eastern bourn,
As though deep down out of the bowels of earth,
Athwart the sky to sink again in the sea.
Where do the Six Dragons[27] have their night berth?
The race beginneth from the dawn of time;
Since man is not the cosmic force,
How could we match its perpetual course?
As grass doth not feel grateful to spring winds for its lush growth,
So nor do the woods bear spite to autumn for their fall of leaves.
Who wieldeth the whip to lash on the run of the seasons!
The rise and fall of all beings are but natural.
Xihe, Xihe[28], why are ye sunk in the expanse of wanton waves?[29]
What virtue was at Luyang's[30] behest his lance to sway,
To make the setting Sun retrace its steps and delay?
It's against heaven's rule to practise trickery for law,
And to massacre the innocent to vaunt brute power[31].
I would enfold the macrocosm all in all,
Superbly 'neath my mind's one lofty pall.[32]

Frontier Tunes

◎ *Li Bai*

(I)

The frontier foes descend in autumnal raids;
Our celestial troops march forth to guard these Han lands.
Our chiefs insignias hold of tiger and bamboo;
Our infantry men lie on the Dragon Sands.
The border moon is curved like a bent bow;
The Hun sky frost on blades of our swords doth fall.
Our Jade Gate Pass hath not been crossed by me,
Young wife of mine, heave thee no sighs at all!

(II)

In June[①] on Mount Tianshan there's naught but snow;
No flowers could be seen, still tarrieth the cold.
Mid tunes of flutes is heard *The Plucking of Willow*,
The vernal hues of Spring are yet to behold
The battles at dawn ensure from drums and gongs,
In nocturnal slumbers I doze off in saddle-hugging,
I would this flashing sword here by my loin,
Be thrust forth straight for the foe Loulan's head-cutting.

---

① The word in the original text is "May", according to the Chinese lunar calendar; "June" in the English version is so translated according to the Gregorian calendar. — Ed.

Plaint on Gem Steps

◎ *Li Bai*

Dew drops on the gem steps fall'n cool
Through her flimsy silken socks seep;
Stepping down through the screen of crystal beads
She at the sparkling autumnal moon doth peep.

For Qing-Ping Tunes[33]

◎ *Li Bai*

(I)

Tinged cloudlets are likened unto her raiment
And the flowers unto her mien.
Spring zephyrs along the balustrade
Gently brush the crystal dew's sheen.
If not seen on the wondrous Mount of Gems
At some enchanted strand,
She could be met with on the Magic Tower
In the moonlit fairyland.

(II)

A spray of fresh pink beauty[34] sparkleth
With dews full of scents sweet;

The clouds and showers of Mount Wu's Belle[35]
Remain today a mere legend.
If it be asked who in the Han palace
Could ever be named as her like,
The answer is "The Flitting Swallow"[36]
In her newly sewn skirt of gauze.

(III)

The Flower famed and the Beauty renowned
Rejoice in each other's note.
They are both smiled upon tenderly
With love by our sovereign lord,
To banish his grief and cares in plenty
From state affairs in the spring breeze,
As they two incline by the balustrade
North of the aloeswood arbour.

Thoughts in a Still Night

◎ *Li Bai*

The luminous moonshine before my bed,
Is thought to be the frost fallen on the ground.
I lift my head to gaze at the cliff moon,
And then bow down to muse on my distant home.

Spring Thoughts

◎ *Li Bai*

When the grasses of Yan[37] are like tufts of green silk in the breeze,
The luxuriant mulberry leaves of Qin[38] hang low on trees.
As thou think of the day when thou wouldst come home from way-
     faring,
I am pining away broken-hearted while lorn fits me seize.
The spring breeze is a stranger altogether unknown to me;
What hast it to do with blowing into my silk curtain piece?

Ziye's Wu Song[39]

◎ *Li Bai*

With moonshine flooding all Chang'an City,
Ten thousand households are clubbing their laundry.
Autumnal winds are blowing all this while,
With yearnings for the Pass of Gem Gateway.
"When could the Huns be subdued for good and aye,
So my goodman could be back from draft far away?"

Long Drawn Yearning[(40)]

◎ *Li Bai*

Ah! long drawn yearning, thither for Chang'an Town!
The katydid is chirping its fall time song
By the well-curb of marble in bas-relief,
While thin frost falleth and mats show warm clime is gone.
The lone and flickering light waneth dim in burning
And my forlorn and dazed thoughts run out nigh;
I turn the lowly hung down curtain up,
To gaze at the moon and heave in vain my sigh.
The Beauteous One[(41)], like a flower beyond the clouds,
Is vaulted above by the empyrean azure,
And by the expanse of clear waves upborne below[(42)].
The skyey distance stretching thus far doth allure
My poor soul to strive so hard in attaining my goal
In its dreams to reach the Border Defile Mount[(43)]!
Ah! long drawn yearning; it gnaweth my heart, — the dole!

Chant over the Stream

◎ *Li Bai*

Aboard a sand pyrus[44] barge with magnolia oars,
Gay players of jade pipes and golden flutes
Mellifluously attune their melodies
At the bow and stern with liquid chords of lutes.
The barque full laden with vintage old and rare,
Along doth bear sonorous belles debonair
To drift wherever listeth the flow of waves.
The fairy flieth down through the azure air[45]
By means of riding astride a yellow crane[46];
The seaboard farer free from wiles his care
Could banish by fixing eyes on the gulls in flight[47].
The radiant odes of Qu Ping's[48] hang ever bright
Throughout the ages to vie with the sun and moon,
But terraces,[49] and arbours built thereon,
Of the kings of Chu could hardly last very long.
When mine ethereal, high mood is on me,
I could wield my brush to shake the Five Noble Mounts,
And as a masterly poem is brought to finish,
I would become elated in spirit to stride
Beyond my hermitage by the waterside.
If worldly glamour were to last forever,
The Stream of Han southeastwards in its flow
Should turn the course northwesterly to go.

River-Crossing Tune

◎ *Li Bai*

'Fore the ferry pavilion the quay-guard greeteth me;
To the east he pointeth to the seaside clouds rising.
For what would you, Master, the river cross?
With such blasts and waves there could be no ferrying.

Humming under the Moon atop the West Tower in Jinling City

◎ *Li Bai*

Mid the silent night in Jinling rising a cool blast,
Up the tower climb I, of Wu and Yue to command my view.
White clouds flashing light on water shake the empty town;
On the autumnal moonshine fall drops of pearly clear dew.
Hum I under the moon, into the depth of the night.
Since the days of old, things are seldom noticed eye to eye:
It is seen the limpid River is calm like tiffany,
Thus reminding one how Xie Tiao[50] his verse doth beautify.

Song of the Emei Mount Peaks Moon

◎ *Li Bai*

Half a disc of that autumnal moon o'er Emei[51] peaks
Throws its bright image into the streams of Pingqiang[52].
Leaving Qingyi[53] for the Three Gorges[54] by night,
I think of, seeing not thee, all the way down to Yuzhou[55].

To Wang Lun

◎ *Li Bai*

Li Bai embarking, just about to depart,
On a sudden heareth tramping and songs and the strand.
The Peach Bloom Deep, a thousand feet in depth,
Runneth not so deep as Wang Lun's thoughts for me command.

Question and Answer in the Mounts

◎ *Li Bai*

Being asked why I retire to the green mounts,
Smiling I reply not with my heart vacant.
Peach blooms and a flowing stream receding far,
Strange are heaven and earth, — a new birth verdant.

Ballad of Mount Lu,[56] Sent to Lord Attendant[57] Lu Xuzhou

◎ *Li Bai*

The lunatic of Chu[58] I am in fact,
Laughing at Confucius[59] with my Phoenix Song.
The Yellow Crane Tower[60] I left at morn,
A fairy's cane of green jade[61] taking along.
Not minding the distances to the Five Mounts[62] fairies to seek,
I all my life like mounts renowned to climb and roam eke.
Mount Lu raiseth its sheer heights fair by the Little Bear[63],
Like nine-folded screens[64] enshrouded in gorgeous clouds of brocade,
Its image in the Lake[65] bright beaming a turquoise rare.
The Two High Cliffs[66] 'fore the Golden Portal Peak[67] tower;
The Silvery Triple Stream[68] from the Three Rock Beams is hung.
The Incense Burner Cataract falleth afar in shower;
Steep crests and folded summits are 'gainst the azure flung.
The rising sun doth its glow on blue tops and scarlet clouds throw;
The flight of birds could not through all the Wu sky[69] go.
Ascending heights to command a broad view of the earth and sky,
I see the great torrential River go on forever.
Sometimes dark clouds for thousands of *li* are ruffled up high,
With snowy waves like heaving hills in nine streams[70] astir.
I like to sing aloud this Mount Lu Ballad;
My feelings for the Mount have risen right glad.
Looking at the Stone Mirror clarifieth my heart;
The whereabouts Sire Xie[71] once loitered is grown with moss.
Taking doses of cinnabar restored[72] in good time
Would purge my mortality, paying bliss rare with cheap loss;

With utmost peace of mind[73], I fairyhood would win,

Espying then fairies floating high up in vermeil clouds,

With lotus blooms in their arms paying homage up the Sacred
　　Mount[74].

I would expect you in advance in the ninth heaven[75],

Greeting you and in your company rove the empyrean.

A Song for Some Friends⁽⁷⁶⁾ on a Dream Trip to Mount Tianmu⁽⁷⁷⁾

◎ *Li Bai*

Mariners speak of the legendary Islands of the Blest⁽⁷⁸⁾, —
Amongst the blown spumes of smoky waves, hard of reach they are
  true.
Yue People speaking of Mount Tianmu are apt to have it thus:
'Neath clouds bedimmed or aglow, it is flashily looming blue.
Tianmu is rolling up sky-high, then running level with it;
It towereth above the Five Great Mounts⁽⁷⁹⁾ and the Crimson Town⁽⁸⁰⁾.
Mount Tiantai⁽⁸¹⁾ known to be one hundred eighty thousand feet high,
Stretching by this, seemeth to be falling southeasterly down.
I would I could through dreaming probe deep into the realm of Yue,
In one night fly past the Mirror Lake's⁽⁸²⁾ reflected lustrous moon.
The lake moon beameth on mine image⁽⁸³⁾,
Watching me flit to the Shan Brook⁽⁸⁴⁾ soon.
There I see Sire Xie's⁽⁸⁵⁾ night hut standing upright still,
Where clear streams flow and flush, and I hear gibbons scream.
Wearing Sire Xie's mountaineering clogs,
I climb flights of steps steep in th' extreme.
Looking eastwards from a crag at the sun on the heaving sea,
I hear the heaven's chanticleer⁽⁸⁶⁾ crowing aloud cock-a-doodle-doo.
Thousands of peaks with innumerable turns I find hard to trace;
Hosts of stray flowers by the rocks I glimpse as dusk falleth to coo.
Bears' growlings and dragon's groanings reverberate through rock dell
  springs
Tremors of fear shake the forests dark and cliffs precipitous.
Clouds bluish are about to sprinkle drops of rain down,

Water is rippling gently as smoke wreatheth soft.

Flash off the lightning jags;

Crash up the thunder-claps;

Pinnacle tops topple headlong;

Avalanches of rocks fall.

A Taoist cave's stone portal is thrown open with a loud bang.

An azure depth yawneth in the bottomless void;

Sun and moon are shooting their splendour on gold and silver spires;

With rainbow gowns and swift blasts as their steeds skyey,

Kinglings of clouds come severally flocking down.

Tigers are plucking in concert on harps heavenly;

Phoenixes are turning round vehicles light and airy.

A host of fairies descendeth all o'er the sky sublimely.

All of a sudden my spirit is quivering, tingling quick[87].

Lost and forlorn, I am frightened out of my dream sighs to heave.

Conscious on my pillow and bedding as I now have come round,

I have lost all those magnificent mountains and plains and lakes.

To fill one's life with rejoicings and jollity is just so;

All things from ancient days are no more than east-flowing water.

Leaving your company fair, when shall I come back north again?

Let my white deer freely graze in the green valleys.

If need be, I would ride it when I feel like to visit renowned mountains.

How could I wrinkle up my forehead and bend my waist to wait on
    those in power,

Making myself crest-fallen for nought?

Parting Thoughts at a Jinling Tavern

◎ *Li Bai*

Spring breeze with willow fluff is filling
The shop with the new brew's sweet odour;
The barmaids fair of Wu are pressing
Fresh wine to urge the guests to savour;
Bright youths of Jinling in twos and threes
Are coming as one to bid me adieu.
The one departing and those who remain,
All drain their stoups for love in lieu.
I beg thee please put questions to
The east-flowing water of the River,
Our farewell yearnings and the stream's,
Which of their cares of parting are stronger?

Seeing Meng Haoran off to Guangling⁽⁸⁸⁾ on the Yellow Crane Tower⁽⁸⁹⁾

◎ *Li Bai*

Mine old friend leaveth the West
From the Yellow Grane Tower.
In this flowery April⁽⁹⁰⁾ clime
For thickly peopled⁽⁹¹⁾ Yangzhou.
A solitary sail's distant speck
Vanisheth in the clear blue:
What could be seen heavenward
Flowing is but the Long River⁽⁹²⁾.

Bidding Adieu to a Friend

◎ *Li Bai*

Across the north suburbs the mounts lie blue,
Around the town's east the stream windeth white.
We are to bid each other here our adieus,
And ye would wander far away ere this night.
Like floating clouds appear the wayfarer's thoughts,
Our friendly feelings seem the sunset glow.
With waves of hands we bid our farewell now.
"Whinny!" doth neigh the departing colt to go.

Bidding Farewell with Feast to Decreed Editor Uncle Yun on Xie Tiao Tower in County Xuan

◎ *Li Bai*

The days having left me, in all those yesterdays
Could not be retained at all;
The days confusing me oft-times nowadays
Are full of worries and gall.
The winds that drive for thousands of *li*
Send autumn's greylags south;
Commanding such a view well suiteth
To drink deep atop this tower.
Your mind is illumed with fairy tracts and classics
Of clairvoyant, happy strain[93],
My thoughts are lit up with glows of poetry afire
With beauty of dazzling vein.
Both you and I are full of buoyant mood
And spirits elevate,
Wishing to fly away ascending the blue
To watch the moon looming great.
One slashing water with the blade of one's sword,
It floweth on all the more;
One raiseth one's goblet to drown one's dolour deep,
And it waxeth doubly sore.
Our life in this insensate, wretched world
Is running counter to our bent;
Tomorrow let's hang up our hats of office[94],
Take to boats on streams in content.

Holding Drink to Ask the Moon[95]

◎ *Li Bai*

"When doth the moon to the blue come?"
I stop my beaker to put the question.
We could not lead or draw on the moon,
Though it moveth along with us to run.
It sparkleth like a flying mirror
O'erlooking the portal cinnabar[96].
The evening haze having subsided,
An ethereal radiance gloweth afar.
We see its rise from the sea at night;
Who knoweth its flight to the clouds at dawn?
The rabbit blanch[97] on the elixir of life
Keepeth on pounding, year in, year out.
With whom doth the fairy lonely dame[98]
As neighbour keep her companion boon?
Our men see not the ancient moon.
Today's moon hath on the ancients shone.
Men ancient and of today like water
That floweth, see the moon thus all.
I would when we sing holding our drink,
The moon its beams to our beakers let fall.

Ascending the Phoenix Terrace[99] of Jinling City

◎ *Li Bai*

On the Phoenix Terrace, phoenixes alighted to play;
They flew off, leaving the empty terrace to overlook
The well-nigh boundless River flowing by itself away.
Wu Palace's[100] flowers and grass have buried the covert paths;
The celebrated courties of Jin[101] are entombed in clay.
The Tri-Peaked Mount[102] is half pointed through the azure sky;
The dual stream[103] the Egret Ait[104] doth fork to splay.
It's all because the floating clouds[105] could cover the sun;
The Imperial City hid from sight[106] doth one dismay.

Sighting the Cataract of Mount Lu

◎ *Li Bai*

The sun shining on the Incense-burner Peak
Issueth purple smoke to wreathe round,
Seen afar the cataract seemeth hung from the cliff top
To the water front of the Mount.
The flying torrent for three thousand feet
Ceaselessly dashing down headlong
Is taken to be the Silvery Stream[1] falling from
The ninth heaven to the ground.

---

① Silvery Stream: The Milky Way.

Ascending Xie Tiao's North Tower[107] at Xuancheng in Autumn

◎ *Li Bai*

The River town like a painted landscape doth shine,
With mountains beaming late in a fair day.
The two entwining streams[108] as mirrors sparkle,
While the pair of bridges[109] like rainbows arch over gay.
With wreaths of cooking smoke arising in the air,
The tangerines and oranges[110] hang in red gold;
All tinges of the scene show fall is far advanced,
As platane leaves look sear and yellow in the cold[111].
Who that ascendeth pensively the North Tower
Doth 'gainst the wind Sire Xie our poet remember[112]?

Embarking from Baidi Town[113] at Early Morn

◎ *Li Bai*

Leaving Baidi on high at dawn
Among the clouds in blaze gay,
A thousand *li* to Jiangling City[114]
I sped within a day.
Unceasingly the gibbons screeched
On both banks of the River,
As my light skiff shot through the folds
Of mounts ten thousand with a whirr.

Looking Back to Olden Times in Yue①

◎ *Li Bai*

When Goujian, King of Yue, had crushed his state foe Wu,
His homing warriors were dressed in brocade all.
The beauties held captive, lush like flowers, thronged the spring court;
Now only partridges are flying and each to each call.

Drinking Alone under the Moon

◎ *Li Bai*

With a jug of wine among the flowers,
I drink alone sans company.
To the moon aloft I raise my cup,
With my shadow to form a group of three.
As the moon doth not drinking ken,
And shadow mine followeth my body,
I keep company with them twain,
While spring is here to make myself merry.
The moon here lingereth while I sing,
I dance and my shadow spreadeth in rout.
When sober I am, we jolly remain,
When drunk I become, we scatter all about.
Let's knit our carefree tie of the good old day;
We may meet above sometime at the Milky Way.

---

① The poet of this quatrain is thinking of the crushing defeat dealt by King Goujian of Yue (越王勾践)
on his mortal foe Fuchai (夫差) and his kingdom of Wu (吴), which was annexed in the year 473 BC.

Sitting in Repose Alone on Jingting Hill

◎ *Li Bai*

All birds have flown up high and far away;
A lonely cloud floated off leisurely.
We gaze at each other to our both fill,
I myself and my hearty Jingting Hill.

A Visit to the Taoist Priest of Daitian Mount without Meeting Him

◎ *Li Bai*

A dog is barking mid the splash of water;
The rain-besprinkled peach blooms appear a pink gay;
'Mongst thickset trees are often sighted deers;
By the runnel, silent are the bells of noonday.
The wild bamboos divide the verdant hue;
A flying spring hangeth down from a green peak.
No one could tell his whereabouts just now;
Nonplussed, I wonder where I could him seek.

Sad, Sad Arbour

◎ *Li Bai*

The grievous spot beneath the sky,
Is the Sad, Sad Arbour for bidding adieu.
The spring breeze knowing farewell's pain,
Giveth not the willow strips a green hue.

Moonlight on the Mount of Borderland Pass

◎ *Li Bai*

The lustrous moon hast risen o'er Mount Sky,
Shedding its sheen midst the sea of clouds up high.
For thousands of *li* wind blasts are being blown
To drive past the Gem Gateway Pass 'neath the sky.
Han troops were sent to battle on the Baideng ways;
The Huns off dared about the Blue Sea banks to pry.
Since olden times from this age-old battle ground,
No one hath been seen to get back home by.
All levied men looking at frontier spots
Would bitterly pine for home with faces wry.
Their mates in storeyed chambers in such nights
Would not e'er cease to heave a sigh after a sigh.

Secluded Gorge Spring

◎ *Li Bai*

Let me wipe that slab of white stone
With the sleeve folds of my loose flowing gown;
I'm to pluck my heptachord plain
By the side of a fresh spring bubbling deep down
In this secluded gorge 'tween mounts twain.
Fair-toned pluckings of fingers deft and apt,
Well directed by my lucid mind and vacant;
Solitary as if lasting a thousand years long,
Like the subdued roarings of a sea of pine foliage
Six score furlongs thick to form a dense throng,
Midst which are to be seen the gibbons sadly shrieking
Self-pityingly, jumping about and clambering
Along precariously atop autumnal trees.
There is one forlorn of hope and bewailing
The times, hearing woe-begone cries such as these,
Who doth flush tears his lapels to drench through.
Thereupon I summon tuneful notes in a gentle flow,
Toning at my finger tips with feelings the melody,
Knowing not, albeit, the sonata thus performed by me
Be ancient or modern. Ah, Secluded Gorge Spring,
In the depth of the forest, it doth sparkle and clearly sing.

Goodman, Cross Ye Not the River[(115)]

◎ *Li Bai*

The Luteous River[(116)] coming from the west

Doth break forth at the foot of Mount Kunlun

To roar for thousands of *li*,

And dash 'gainst the Gate of Dragon[(117)].

Its waves ran tossing their white crests at the skies,

To make *Di* Yao in grieving heave his sighs.

Thereupon Great Yu conducted hundreds of streams

To flush to the east in their tumultuous flow

(He bypassed thrice his home in thirteen years)[(118)],

Subduing cataracts, suppressing the flood,

For the Nine States to settle down to till and sow[(119)].

When the calamitous deluge was over,

There still remain the stormy sand gusts to blow.

A wild-miened madman, spreading his hoary hair

In the blasts, what would he do, in face of the river?

The onlookers would heed not what he doeth.

But his own mate up steppeth to stop her man:

"My goodman, cross ye not the river, refrain!

Ye might as well go with a tiger to grapple,

But wade ye not the river torrents main;

If ye be drowned and drifted to some far-off shore,

There'd be giant whales with white teeth like snowy peaks;

My goodman, ye'd be wound up high o'er there.

Just as the zither's plaint sore, — home, no more!"

Epistolet Inviting My Cousins to a Spring Night Banquet in the Garden of Peach Blossoms

◎ *Li Bai*

As heaven and earth form the caravansary[1] of all beings, so one's span of mortality is a transient guest of millenniums. Our floating life is like a dream: how scanty are its joys! That is the reason why there were men of old lighting lanterns to illuminate their night ramblings. Moreover, Spring summons us with her splendid landscape and Nature lends us his brave[2] masterpiece. Gathering in the fair garden of peach blossoms to exchange our natural brotherly love, we would make a boon company of talented youths. The songs you will sing actuated by your superior gifts would put me your elder cousin to shame. Before the appreciative epithets of the scene would cease, our elevated converse[3] would rise to a pure (-tenored Lao-Zhuang) metaphysical discourse. Superb banquet would be spread while we sit at the table enjoying the flowers, and winged beakers would be given flight to between one anther in sousing while we gaze at the moon. Without subtile writings, how could we express our exquisite fleelings? If any one of us faileth to compose a poem, three bumpers would fall to his lot by enforcement.

---

[1] caravansary: inn with a large inner courtyard where caravans put up in Eastern countries; khan.
[2] brave: excellent; splendid.
[3] converse: conversation (old use).

Song of Farewell Sung in Jinling for Fan Xuan

◎ *Li Bai*

The Rocky Mount its cliffs like a squatting tiger[120] doth rear,
O'erlooking the waves as for to cross the river blue.
The chain of Zhong Heights windeth up twisting as a dragon.
To share with the trees of Liyang in their verdant hue.
For autumns three hundred, o'er forty ruling *di*[121],
Their events and glories have all ebbed with the east flowing stream.
The boy astride a white horse tall, — what could he be?[122]
The yielder-rebel in Taiqing years, of crime extreme.
How fame and honour redound to Jinling's splendid past!
All the renowned and heroic had come to its demesne old.
Now all the lordly and notable are turned into smoke and fog,
Quadrigas golden and chairs of gem have become ashes cold,
I sigh and shout in vain, while striking my sword blade:
Skeletons of Liang and Chen were rank like heaps of cut broom.
The Emperor had sunk down the Jingyang court well[123];
Who was to sing the "Palace Rear Yard Jade-Tree Bloom"?
This place is heart-wringing beyond the saying of words;
It is now grown with hanging down, tall weeds of spring;
I see thee off with regret like this River of thousands of *li*;
Let some future year, to see a Hoary Recluse[124], back thee bring.

Descending from Mount Zhongnan[125], Putting up at the Mountaineer Husi's[126] Lodging and Being Entertained with Drinking

◎ *Li Bai*

Towards the dusk as I come down from the verdant heights,
The mountain moon is following me closely along.
When I look backwards at the trail just passed through now,
How emerald green beams the mountainside's sloping lawn!
Encountering my host, I am led to his rustic home;
His youngsters open the brushwood doors with cheer smiling,
The bamboo grove unfoldeth a shade secluded path;
The hanging usnea whorls rustle against the pedestrians'clothing.
With kindly words, I am given bed and offered good fares,
As well as mellow wine in bumpers for toast to raise.
We sing the "Song of Winds into the Pine Forest Blown";[127]
When we finish, stars in the Silvery Stream grow dim in their gaze.
I become drunk and you go talkative and boon,
We both are set quite free from the bounded ego of our own.

Yellow Crane Tower

◎ *Cui Hao*[1]

The man of fairy lore hath gone
By riding a yellow crane,
So here is but left the tower called
The Yellow Crane by name.
The yellow crane hath flied away
Not to come back again,
For a thousand years there are white clouds
Floating in the blue void main.
The sun on the fair-day river shineth
And on trees of Hanyang Town[(128)]
The sweet verdure on the Parrot Isle[(129)]
Is beaming a lush, fresh lawn.
In the setting sun's light where could be
The native pass of the borough?
The smoky spumes on the River's surface
Fill the onlookers with sorrow.

---

[1] Cui Hao (704? – 754), a talented poet. His *Yellow Crane Tower* is the best among all the poems on the same topic.

Sighting the Great Mount Dai

◎ *Du Fu*[1]

How is the magnificent Mount Dai[(130)]?
A boundless mass of green peaks and cliffs
Towering over the states Qi and Lu.
Nature doth summon here Wondrous Beauty;
Thus Light and Shade[(131)] could divide and part.
The cumulus doth broaden one's breast;
'T would split one's eyelids to watch homing birds.
Some day I must climb up to the top,
To look down viewing all the peaks small.

---

[1] Du Fu (712 – 770), courtesy name Zimei and style name Shaoling, a prominent poet of the Tang Dynasty. Along with Li Bai, he is frequently called the greatest of the Chinese poets. He had a strong sense of history, and his poems were praised as "history in poetic forms". He was also the synthesizer of regulated forms of traditional Chinese poetry.

Chief of Corps Fang's Steed of the Huns

◎ *Du Fu*

The Hun clans steed of Dayuan fame
Is stalwart, spare in build,
With ears like whittled bamboo flukes sharp,
And hoofs wind-borne and -filled.
Where'er it fareth, there's no breadth;
Your life and death may entrust to it ye,
As, brave and dauntless is it thus,
Ten thousand *li* it speedeth in a spree.

A Hawk Portrayed

◎ *Du Fu*

Frosty winds arise from the sheet of silk white;
Drawn, a hawk is nonpareil, vivacious, true,
Heaving up in perch, with thoughts of hares wild,
Turning eyes aslant, like an ape in deep rue.
Silken cords and metal frame both shine bright,
At the hall pillar whereon the picture is hung.
Would these talons were to thrash ill, vile fowls,
To make their sickly blood and feathers on sod flung.

The Rime of the War-Chariots

◎ *Du Fu*

Rumble the chariots, neigh and snort the horses,

Men of arms with bows and arrows all hung

Dazzlingly athwart their both flanks and hips,

March alongside with parents, wives and children;

Dusts are trampled up, the Xianyang Bridge from sight hid.

Dragging clothes and stamping feet, the files they clutter,

Cries and clamours rising skyward they utter.

Passers-by ask the marching men of their condition;

The raw recruits say incessant is the conscription.

Some from fifteen are drafted north the River to fend,

Till at forty they are sent west border farms to tend.

When departing, ward leaders wound turbans round their heads,

Coming back hoary, they are sent to the borderland.

On the frontiers bloodshed flusheth to form seas of gore;

Emperor Wu yet aimeth his domain to expand.

See you not in the two hundred Han counties east of the Mount,

Thousands of villages and hamlets are choked with brambles and
    thorns?

Though there be hardy women to wield the hoes and ploughs,

Corn groweth scattered on plots and in fields devoid of rows.

Since we Qin recruits are inured to hard fought battles,

We are driven to fight like cocks and dogs amain.

Though you elders are concerned to question us,

How do we conscript men dare to show our bile vain?

Take for instance what is happening this winter.

Not at all is enlisting west of the Pass let free.

Magistrates are pressing for taxes in kind hard;

Where should they come from? What are they to be?
Plain it is, giving birth to boys is a curse,
Not comparable to bearing daughters at all.
Daughters could be married to some neighbours,
Sons would only lie buried under the grasses tall.
See you not on the distant shores of the Blue Sea,
Bones of those who fell down long ago lie bleaching,
New ghosts wail in company with those of old,
Under a dreary sky, rain drizzling and wind screeching.

Song on the Eight Faeries in Drinking[132]

◎ *Du Fu*

Zhizhang[133] rideth his horse like sitting aboard on tossing waves;
Dazed in sight and fallen down a well, he dozeth on.
The Prince of Ruyang[134] would attend his Sovereign's morning court
Only after taking three big bumpers of drinks strong;
Meeting wheeled tanks of liquors on the way, saliva would he flow,
Grieved that he is not ordained the fief of Wine Spring.
Li the Left Chancellor[135], spending ten thousand coins daily,
Draweth scores of streams like a giant whale in his drinking,
Relishing cups in these sage times, giving place to Virtue.
Zongzhi[136], lively, refined, the flower of youthful manliness,
Raiseth stoups with his pupils white glinting at the gross common[137],
Turning his sight to the radiant azure, graceful, matchless,
Splendid like a jade tree waving in spree fore heaven's winds.
Su Jin[138] the vegetarian, facing Buddha's portrait,
Oft his dhyana vigils faileth to keep when drunk he be.
Li Bai[139] poureth forth a hundred poems after a quart's weight,
Falling asleep in a public house in Chang'an the chief town,
Waving aside th' Son of Heavens summons to appear,
Saying he himself is a faery in th' realm of spirits.
Zhang Xu[140], famed as th' *cao* mode calligraphic art's seer,
Taking off his hat after three huge mugs fore th' king and lords,
Waveth brushes across scrolls like flights of smoke and cloud.
Jiao Sui[141] beameth bright after five full horns of liquid fire,
Talking, arguing fervidly, with wonder his company doth shroud.

The Lay of the Belles[142]

◎ *Du Fu*

On the Third Moon's Third Day[143], while fresh is the clime,

On Chang'an's bund, there belles are a good many,

Of graces rich and rare, in virtue, chaste, pure[144],

In flesh and bones, well matched, in aspect, dainty.

Their broidered taffeta vestures shine in late spring,

With gold-thread phoenixes[145] and unicorns[146] in silver.

And what are decked on their comely heads?

With emerald gems, down to temples, of multi-layer[147].

And what are espied behind their backs?

With pearl-studded bands[148], around their waist lines curving.

Amongst them are the Doted-on One's sisters fair,

Entitled the State Queens of Han and Guo and Qin[149].

For victuals, they choose camel hump stew in apphrine jugs,

And shining fish fresh steamed on crystal platters.

Being satiated, they keep held back for long

Their chopsticks of rhinoceros's horn, as cutters

Of their maids with tinkling bells[150] bustle about in vain.

The eunuchs let fly their reins without stirring up dust,

The imperial kitchen sending the choice eight with silk nets.

All the pipes and tabours play in concord with gust,

While guests and attendants hustle to their noted alcoves.

And last, up cometh a wavering, saddled horse[151],

Its rider, dismounting at the platform, stalketh

By a short front path through the lush shrubs of gorse,

Direct (via the hall) to the brocade-cushioned parlour.

The willow catkins on the marsileas white

Are falling thick; blue birds are making flight

With kerchiefs red in their bills to show amour's troth[152],

His mighty power's hot air could your hands sear;

Beware, come not near, the Chancellor would be wroth.

The Lay of Meipi[153]

◎ *Du Fu*

Fond of wonders are the Cen Shen[154] brothers,
Taking me afar for this trip to Meipi.
Of a sudden heaven and earth their colours change;
Waves torrential heave on th' expanse of a glazy sea.
Boundless swells our barque is tossed by and buoyed up on;
Strange 'tis, grieved am I[155] while full excited too:
Alligators in craze and whales in gulp fits
Heed I not; wild gusts, foamy heaves, with me nor ado.
All at once, the chief boatman hoisteth his silken sails,
Right glad is the crew, as blown o'er is the squall,
Scattered are the water fowls, while the boat songs
Ring out loud, the strings and flutes aboard enthrall
All the emerald of the hillsides wide around.
Deep is probed the sounding pole to test in vain;
Leaves of trapa and lotus flowers seem washed clean.
While in midstream, limpid blue is it like the main,
Down 'neath Zhongnan's foot, its mass loometh jet black.
In the southern half of Meipi is steeped
Deep the shadowed south mount, its wavering image
Silhouetted and fluctuating 'gainst white clouds heaped.
Th' shallop bow, reflected, hitteth th' bonzary
Cloud-girt; a mirrored moon ariseth up Blue Field Pass.
Thereon, ebon dragons spew forth their pearls,
As Fengyi, God of Luteous River, his drum of brass
Beateth, to summon them; Xiang queens and Han sprites all appear
Singing and dancing, while golden boughs and green flags
Plumed with king-fisher's feather flash and darken clear.
Swiftly, fear-stricken, I were caught in a thunder-storm:
Unpredictable is the will of divinity.
How could youth retard the approach of old age?
Joy and sorrow fill the sack of infinity!

A Moonlit Night[(156)]

◎ *Du Fu*

The moon tonight at Fuzhou
Is but seen alone in her chamber.
A pity 'tis to me, so far
Away here, to think our children
Not yet know how Chang'an to remember.
Her cloudy coiffure is moistened
By a mist of odorous flavour;
The moon's fair lustre is cooling
Her gem-hued arms to deliver
A shapely curvature.
I wonder when I'd stand with her
By the gauzy curtain drapery,
To let moon beams shine and quiver
On our teary stains to dry them
Off slowly both together.

Spring Prospects⁽¹⁵⁷⁾

◎ *Du Fu*

The state being broken up,
Its mounts and streams remain.
The capital in spring
Doth thickly plants contain.
Aggrieved by the times' events,
On flowers I shed my tears;
With regrets for enforced partings,
The birds' songs stir up my fears.
Midst flares of war for three moons,
Home letters seem a huge sum.
Mine hoary hair's scratched so thin,
This hairpin would slip through the thrum.

Qiang Village[158]
(Three Poems)

◎ *Du Fu*

(I)

Like red cliffs, clouds are towering in the west;
The fiery feet of the sun are stepping on the plain.
On bramble doors the sparrows twitter loud;
The homeward wayfarer his trek's end doth gain.
My mate and young, surprised at my being alive,
Their tears all wipe after moment's daze and stun.
Amidst these turmoils, suffering such disasters,
I've come back; what a chance is this fateful one[159]!
Our neighbours gather crowding atop the walls[160],
Being struck, astounded, heaving sighs in plenty;
All night we spend in candle light till dawn,
Bemused, as each to each in dreams doth pry.

(II)

Enforced to live as by stealth in these late years[161]
I come back home without any much good humour.
My children dear their father's knees seldom leave,
For fear I would soon depart at some late hour.
I could recall how airing I liked in the past[162],
Being used to walk all round the trees by the pond,
While roaringly blew the gusts of northerly winds,
I brooded on all what had happened that made me despond.

With hap, the grains are in good time reaped and threshed,
And the wine press is properly worked on for brew.
Now that there would be enough supply of drinks,
For me to console old age and with warmth endue.

(III)

On the guest's arrival, the fighting village cocks[163]
Are crowing one and all in a wild uproar;
They are all driven up to roost on the trees[164],
And then is heard the knocking on the bramble door.
The village elders, four or five of them,
All come for my trek so far-off and long, me to cheer,
They take along with them severally one and all,
And pour out tankards of drinks or turbid or clear,
Apologizing[165] for the wine's sore lack of strength,
For the millet fields are lacking hands to till,
As the punitive draftings are yet continued on,
The boys[166] are all enlisted for the eastward drive still.
"Your kind dear thoughts for me do deeply touch me;
Please let me sing for you, village elders, dear."
When I have finished, facing the sky I heave sights;
All round me, tears do flush, making all eyes blear.

To the Eighth Wei Brother, the Anchorite

◎ *Du Fu*

Two friends oft sighting not each other in life
Are like the stars Antares and Betelgeuse[167].
What a night is this serene and gracious one
For us in the gentle candle sheen from cares to break loose!
How long could one remain still young and strong?
Our crown and temporal tufts are growing hoar,
And 'tis known some half of our old friends 've become ghosts,
Distressed and grieving, we exclaim both sore.
How could I know after all these twenty years
I come to visit again your lustrous hall?
When I saw you last, you were not married yet;
Today you are surrounded by girls and boys tall.
In blandness they regards to their elder pay,
Inquiring me whence I do hither hail.
Before the genial converse is drawn to a close,
Your boys and girls afford sweet drinks and cocktail.
Mid even drizzles, they cut odorous allium of spring,
The new-husked rice is cooked with millet choice.
Mine host laying stress on the difficulty of meeting,
Proposeth toasts full then on end to rejoice.
With stoups full ten I am not yet at all drunk,
Still I thank you heartily for your old time zeal.
Tomorrow we shall be severed again by mount chains
And hosts of mundane matters noisy peal.

Xin'an Officer[168]

◎ *Du Fu*

While trudging on the high way toward[169] Xin'an,
One heard the tumult of recruits' roll call.
The chief officer of Xin'an was thus asked:
"Is none of age[170], your district being small?"
"Ordaining that the middle class[171] be listed,
The draughting order yesternight came down."
"The middle ones are still too undersized;
How could they well defend the Royal Town[172]?"
Stout boys were taken leave of by their mothers;
Lean ones, beloved by none, departed alone[173].
As white the stream did eastward flow ere eve,
The verdant hills still echoed with dear ones' moan.[174]
"Let not your eyes be quite exhausted till shrunk;[175]
Restrain your tears too flushed to over-brimming!
Your eyes when shriveled would expose their sockets;
Alack! that Heaven and Earth[176] are void of feeling!
Our troops Imperial aim to take Xiangzhou city;
By morn or night, we look forth the campaign to win;
But unexpected are the rebels' tactics[177],
And our men are not subject to one supreme discipline[178].
Yet with food supplies not far away at the base[179],
Their training center is quite near the capital late[180];
They'd dig their ditches not deep enough to find water[181];
In grazing horses, their labour is also not great.
What's more, the cause of our armed might is upright[182],
Our officers in command are strict yet kind.
Let those who see the recruits off be not sorely sad;
The deputy chancellor[183] holdeth you all in his mind."

The Shihao Officers[(184)]

◎ *Du Fu*

At dusk I put up at the hamlet Shihao[(185)]
Where officers were pressing men to enlist.
An old man fled by clambering the wall;
His wife went forth to answer the front door shouts.
How angry were the officer's mad howls!
How wretched were the woman's plaintive cries!
I heard then what she said in these her words:
"My three sons went to guard the city Ye[(186)]
Of whom, one sent his message some days ago:
The other two were killed few days before.
The live one is to lead his life by stealth;
The two dead ones are blotted out for good!
There is no one else in this ill-fated room,
But mine infantile, still-its-ma's-milk-sucking grandson,
With its ma staying with me to care for it;
So poor we are, she weareth her skirt in rags.
Although both weak and aged I am by now,
I may still go with you officers to serve,
At the Heyang[(187)] encounter forth-coming,
For getting ready the breakfast for our troops."
As deep the night grew, she was no more heard;
Beseemeth it that sobs and weeping did sound.
At daybreak forging ahead for my forward trudge,
I bade adieu to the old man alone[(188)].

Tong Pass[189] Officer[190]

◎ *Du Fu*

How weary do the rank and file appear,
While building walls along the way to Tong Pass!
The bulwark huge than iron is more stalwart;
The citadel small ten thousand feet doth surpass[191].
The Tong Pass Officer is queried by me:
"Is strengthening the Pass still[192] to ward off the Tartars?"
I am then asked to dismount and look around,
Being shown about the verge of the peaks sparse:
"Up high in the clouds are ranged the palisades[193],
Which fleeting birds cannot even fly across.
Whene'er the Tartars come, but keep on guard,
Be carefree from the western capital's[194] loss.
Look thither, Sir, at those strategic straits,
Precipitous and narrow, single cart's tracks;
By wielding a long-shafted halberd[195] strong,
A hardy warrior could repel all attacks."
"Alas! the calamitous Taolin defeat[196],
When our men, a million, earthworms to fish became.
Please charge our generals in guard of the Pass,
To follow Geshu's example, never aim!"

Parting after Nuptials[(197)]

◎ *Du Fu*

The dodder cleaving to the raspberry
And flax[(198)], its tendrils cannot thus be long;
To marry off one's girls to wayfarers
Is worse than casting them off the wayside along.
To be thy mate and wife fore'er and aye,
I share with thee thy bed not till 'tis warm.
Our nuptials erst by eve and parting at morn, —
To our union, is it not like thunder and storm?
Although thou goeth away not very far,
To guard the border and at Heyang quite near,
My station[(199)] here at home is not yet plain;
How shall I hold my in-laws[(200)] to be mine dear?
My parents reared me with solicitous care,
Safeguarding me from touch with tricks of ill fate[(201)].
A girl once born would finally home by her lot;
She hath to nestle on her wedlock ultimate[(202)].
Since thou art now on the way to peril of death,
Sore pain is wringing hard mine heart and bowels!
Though I swear to follow thee where thou art going,
The shape of things preventeth my wish with scowls.
So mind thee not our new, dear cherished wedding,
But pay good heed to the warfare going on.
To have in the camps enlistees feminine,
The troops' morale would perhaps be soddened down.
I sigh for being a girl of a family poor;
It taketh me long to sew these stuffed clothes silken;
But padded garments of silk I stop to wear,
And for thy sake, I rouge and powder shun.
In looking up, I see all birds that fly;
Those large and small must hover by twos and twos.
Our human affairs are often wretched, awry;
But I look forward to be with thee, my spouse[(203)]!

Parting during Declining Years⁽²⁰⁴⁾

◎ *Du Fu*

The suburbia⁽²⁰⁵⁾ from chaos not yet free,
A man thus cannot peace enjoy while old.
With offspring all in battles fallen and gone,
Why need a wretched man his life to hold?
In throwing off his staff and leaving home,
He hath his compeers all for him feel sorry.
Though being lucky to have his teeth intact,
He's sad his marrow hath been shrunk and dry.
Since the man hath put on helmet and coat-of-mail,
He hath to salute his superior and depart.
His old helpmate by roadside doth lie and wail,
As the year is drawing to close and sore is her heart.
He knoweth well this is their death-parting nonce,
And grieveth her clothes too thin for the sharp chill.
This parting will have certainly no return,
Yet he is told to increase his daily meals still.
The fort of Tumen⁽²⁰⁶⁾ hath been strongly built,
And Apricot Orchard Town⁽²⁰⁷⁾ is hard to pass through,
As things are not like the City of Ye's break-up,
Though I'd end in death, yet that I'd go to slow.
When Fate hath destined a couple to go apart,
One cannot choose between or youth or age.
Recalling all those peace-blest days of yore,
One could but sigh and dote on that parted stage.
Now that encounter and fortressing are rampant,
War flames o'er all the chain of mounts are flaring.
The corpses have left grass lands and woods all rank,
The streams and plains are all dyed gory by bleeding
Ah! where is to be found the land of bliss?
Why should I hesitate and linger on!
So, let me give up this humble thatched cottage,
And torn asunder is my heart anon.

Parting sans a Home[(208)]

◎ *Du Fu*

Lorn and blighted since the Tianbao Period,
Gardens, cottages, all grow lush with wild weeds.
O'er a hundred families of my homeland
Have been scattered all about by the rebel deeds.
Those who are living are without tidings,
Others that are dead have become dust and clay.
Piteous, poor me, back from Xiangzhou's bad rout,
Come I here to trace mine used past life's way.
After a long walk, reaching an empty lane, where
Beams of the sun are scant, the air is dreary,
I see foxes two and three, all staring,
Bristling their hair in wrath and screeching at me.
What are there, in the neighbourhood all around thither?
One or two old wives now widowed, reft of hope.
Nestling birds all cherish twigs of their own nests;
People could not but choose to live in their used scope.
During this springtide tillage, I wield the hoe alone;
Toward sun down, I water the vegetable patch small.
Just then having heard of my returning home,
The *Xian* officer summoneth me with a call
To drill the draftees as their corporal drummer.
Though enlisted am I now locally in this state,
There is no one, nor a home for me to part from;
Going far off, I hold no hope of homing late.
As home and native land are all wiped clean off,
There is no difference 'twixt what's far and what's near.
Ever heart-broken, mourn I my long ill mother,
Five years since, she died in poverty sheer.
Birth she did give me, yet to her 'tis of no avail,
To her, as to me, bitter it proveth ever.
Now that one hath not even a home to part from,
How could one the lot of a subject suffer?

The Beauty[209]

◎ *Du Fu*

A peerless beauty there doth reside
In a solitary abode in a dell.
She sayeth she erst came of high birth,
But haplessly by the woods here doth dwell.
"Within the Pass[210] there was unrest;
My brothers have been ruthlessly killed.
Their station high was of no avail;
Their mortal remains are not buried as willed.
The ways of the world dislike ill-luck;
All things decline and bear fate to hem.
My goodman is a light, fickle one;
His new mated bride is fair like a gem.
The rose mallows[211] their time all know;
The mandarin ducks roost not alone.
He seeth his new won bride's smile sweet,
But heareth not the old one's sad groan."
The mountain springs are clear and pure;
When they flow outward, turbid they grow.[212]
Her maid, returning from selling her pearls,
Is mending the thatch with ivy bough.
She plucketh flowers not to deck her hair,
But filleth cypress leaves her palms' scoops all.
In this chill air with green sleeves thin,
She leaneth at dusk on a bamboo tall.

Two Poems on Dreaming of Li Bai(213)

◎ *Du Fu*

(I)

Severance by death is choking in sorrow;

Parting during lifetime grieveth one deep!

South of the River hath been pestilence stricken;

Exiles there are scanter of news than tide neap.

Mine old friend my dream did enter last night;

Plain it is for I thought of him in earnest.

Doubt I harbour, it be your soul ethereal;

Far off, I know not it is your spirit manifest.

Your soul cometh afar hithcr from where maples are green,

Whither you'd go back from here full of passes black.

Now that you are caught in coiled nets intricate,

How could you fly hither fleetly on wings with knack?

The setting moon's sheen is spread on the beams of my room;

Vivid mien of his seemeth still shined upon clear.

Deep is the flood and broadly the huge waves upheave;

Watch out, let not sharks and dragons to you come near.

(II)

Clouds afloat are drifting along all day long;

So our wanderer cometh not back us to see.

Dreams I had of you for three nights on end;

Plain it is how your feelings are for me.

So reluctant was your farewell bidding mode,

Saying how thus difficult 'twas for you to come:

Bodies of waters are oft swept by winds and squalls,
Boating trips are then too apt to be troublesome.
Scratching his hoary head the while, he my door left,
As if having failed to fulfill his cherished will.
Hatted high officials[214] throng the capital;
Such a fine man alone is wretched yet still!
Who sayeth Heaven's law of justice kindly be?
Verging to age, he's tormented yet by ill hap!
Fame immortal is to be his future lot;
Lonelily would he enjoy it across the eternal gap.

For Li Bai(215)

◎ *Du Fu*

Since the coming of autumn, we both do still wander in vain,
Availing ourselves nought with cinnabar to follow Gehong;
Why with drinkings hard and singings wild to spend days,
Do you fly defiant and haughty, for whom be so high-flown?

Longing for My Younger Brothers(216) in a Moolight Night

◎ *Du Fu*

The garrison's curfew drums have cleared the streets;
An autumn brant is heard in its border-flight screams.
The crystal dews are chilling from tonight forth;
Our moon at home is solely brighter in its gleams.
My brothers all are scattered wide o'er the land;
I have no home now to know of their life and death.
All messages sent astray could reach them nought,
Whenas the campaign is still in its full breadth.

Riverside Village[217]

◎ *Du Fu*

A curve of limpid stream embracing round doth flow;
In this long summer day's bank village all is quiet:
The swallows come and go by themselves high up in my hall;
The gulls on the water bill and coo with love beset.
Mine elderly mate draweth lines on paper for a checkerboard;
Our little boy striketh a needle to make a fishing hook.
If there but be old friends to supply me their office rice,
What doth my humble self care, for something else to look?

The Crazy Man[218]

◎ *Du Fu*

A thatched cot lieth in th' west of Ten-thousand-*li* Bridge[219],
By th' Multiflorous Pond[220] that's my clear Canglang[221] Stream.
While breezes cherish dainty bamboo pipes green and cute,
The lotus blooms pink, imbued with sprinkles, scent sweet and gleam.
The letters of a friend with heavy sovran bestowals[222] cease to come;
Mine ever hungry children's faces grow drear and sad.
To be starved to death and be thrown to th' canyons, one should be
   defiant[223];
I laugh at myself while getting old being e'er more mad[224].

Arrival of a Guest[(225)]

◎ *Du Fu*

Enfolded in the north and south with spring bourns,
From my thatched hall I see the gulls[①] by day.
My flower paths have not been swept for guests;
These shrub-strung doors are opened first on your way.
My victuals are plain, for I stay away from town;
This stoup of wine, as I'm poor, is an old brew.
Care ye to drink with the good old neighbour of mine?
I'll ask him to come and share our residue.

Glad at Raining in a Spring Night

◎ *Du Fu*

Gracious raining knoweth its timely season;
Down it cometh promptly during springtide.
Following breezes it slinketh by at nightfall,
Things to soothe, minutely, mutely to bide.
Topping with paths, clouds amass to loom black.
Lights on a river barque alone do shine bright.
Look ye by dawn wherever red and moistened:
Flowers blow the Brocade-robed Officials' Town with delight.

---

① See note (47) of Li Bai's poem *Song on the River* (《江上吟》).

Song on My Cottage Being Broken by Autumnal Blasts[(226)]

◎ *Du Fu*

The autumnal vault of heaven is arching high
As September's blasts are roaring loud;
They blow away the three-fold layers of reeds
That the bulrush thatch of my house enshroud.
The reeds are blown across the river flow
And scattered along the waterside;
Some masses hung up high as caught atop
A number of brushwood brambles by the tide,
While others whirled and flung low down to float
Or, submerged in ponds and stuck in mires, lay.
A pack of the southern village urchins taking
Advantage of mine old age and decay,
Are brazen enough to play the brigands bold;
They barefacedly snatch up and speed away
The bunches of reeds into the bamboo groves thick,
Despite mine hoarse exhorting 'gainst their tricks;
So I could but come back to lean on my cane
And heave vain sighs and cry alack!
Ere long the blasts are blown over and still,
The blue dome is covered with clouds jet black.
My cloth bed quilt, after many years of use,
Is cold and hard like an iron sheet,
Being kicked and stamped to be full of holes by my boys
In their naughty sleep and dreams with feet.
On my bed the drips of rain leak down from the roof

Like tufts of hemp incessant and fleet.
Ever since the rebel uprising, I have been
Devoid of calm and restful sleep.
When would this chilly, wet and dolorous night
Come to its end at a bright, fair peep?
How could there be great hosts of mansions broad
To shelter and cheer up scholars all over,
Where they may live as calmly as mountaintops,
With nor wind blasts nor drips to deter!
Alas!
If all of a sudden appeareth such a sight,
Then, mine hut be broken and I be frozen to death,
I would take that as of little concern and light.

A Quatrain on the Crimes of the Court Brigades[227]

◎ *Du Fu*

Although the warriors of the court are brave,
They ravage and debauch no less than our hated foes.
Well known to all are their murders on the Han Stream,
And women are rounded up by them as camp whores.

A Quatrain

◎ *Du Fu*

Two yellow orioles atop th' green willows sing,
A row of egrets white ascends the sky pale blue.
My casement frames th' west mounts capped with perennial snow,
Outdoors my house are moored ships thousands of *li* from East Wu.

Two Quatrains[(228)]

◎ *Du Fu*

(I)

Under the slowly moving sun,
The streams and hills with beauty abound;
As blown by breezes of the sparkling spring,
All flowers and herbs sweet scents spread around.
The clay erst frozen waxing soft now,
Is pecked by swallows their nests to make;
The sandy bank of the ait being warm,
Along it paired mandarin ducks dozes take.

(II) A

The river being blue, all the more
The water fowls look dazzlingly white.
The hills lie verdant stretching along,
The flowers on them are burning bright.
It seems this spring ere long would be gone,
As the last several ones, once more;
Alas, what day would it be then,
As I wish to be at home so sore?

(II) B

— the variant version of this poem —

The River blue doth make the fowls look whiter;
The hillock green doth show its flowers burning.
This spring appeareth to have passed its prime;
When shall be the year I could go home, returning?

73

Yu's Temple[(229)]

◎ *Du Fu*

In Great Yu's temple up high in th' vacant mounts,
Autumnal wind on th' slanting sun's shine blows;
In its desolate court aloft hang citrus fruits;
On th' walls are spread the dragons and snakes frescoes.
While clouds are issuing out of hollowed crags,
Th' resounding river waves on th' white sands roll.
Well known it has been, he rode the four vehicles[(230)],
To conduct and dig, for the Three Ba's control.

Eight Octaves on Autumnal Musings [(231)]

◎ *Du Fu*

(I) [(232)]

Chill, crystal dews have seared the maple woods;

The aura of the Wu Mounts and Gorges is drear.

While waves of the flood upheave against the sky,

Dense wind-swept clouds unfurl to shroud the peaks sheer.

Chrysanthemums have bloomed twice with my tears of the past;

To a single boat are cleaving my thoughts nostalgic.

The need of winter garments is urgent all round;

In Baidi aloft, the eve laundry clubbings sound thick.

(II) [(233)]

When the sun inclineth west at Kuizhou the lone town,

I use to yearn for the capital neath the Great Bear.

With tears bedewed at three sad wails of gibbons,

In vain I aim on the raft toward heaven to repair.

Prevented by illness the secretariat to attend,

By the mountain tower's limed wall I list the pipe sorry.

Please look at the moon beams cast on the wisteria o'er the stones,

Reflecting their light on th' isle rush flowers hoary.

(III) [(234)]

In the thousand homes' mount town in morn sun calm,

For days I view aloft the rolling green;

While night after night the fishing boats float along,

To and fro autumn swallows flit about in the scene.
Like Kuang Heng, I dissented but thus fare ill;
Following Liu Xiang's example, I yet fail in mine aim:
As my fellow students of yore with joy do thrill,
Those favoured ones all prosper in wealth and fame.

(IV)[235]

I've heard that things in Chang'an are like chess games;
Its events these tens of years are seethed with sorrow.
The princely, noble mansions have new masters;
All civil and martial chiefs are none of years ago.
Right north from passes of mounts, reports of fights din;
The messages of westward campaigns in fights do flee. —
Like fish and dragons, neath autumn river cold,
I think of my native soil as an absentee.

(V)[236]

The Penglai palatial mansions face the South Mounts;
A Golden Pillar riseth upright toward the sky.
High up from Gem Pool in the west, descendeth Dame Wang;
From th' east a purple aura the Han Pass doth sanctify.
Like clouds the fans of pheasant-tail plumes move to ope;
Dawn beams on the dragon robe reveal His mien. —
Lying by neath the flood, I am surprised 'tis so late;
How oft I was roll-called at the portal carved in green.

(VI)[237]

The Qutang Gorge mouth and Zigzag River bank,
Though far apart, are joined in autumn's war fires.
From Flower-sepals Tower, led th' imperial path;

To Hibiscus Garden, went sad news of border pyres.
An alighting swan would be enclosed by towers;
While gulls in flight would be startled by masts and riggings.
But look back! what a pity is the site of dance and song;
This old terrain is from ages past the land of our kings.

(VII)[(238)]

The Kunming Lake's expanse was dug in Han;
Its flags and banners of Wu-*di* appear still waving.
That Shuttle Girl applieth not moonlit nights;
A jade whale its fins in autumn wind seem wafting.
The zizania fluttered by waves are dense like clouds;
The lotus cupules shivered by dews withered are. —
The clift pass so precipitous is but birds' path;
A fisherman lone and lorn, I have wandered far.

(VIII)[(239)]

The way through Kunwu and Yusu circuitous is;
Via Purple Pavilion Peak's shade, one reacheth Meipi.
The grains of fragrant rice are by parrots' pecks left;
Firmiana branches green, long by phoenixes perched be.
Fair youths in springtide outing, gifts exchange;
Companions fairy share their boats till deep in night. —
In the past, my pictorial brush hath touched his Grandeur;
Expecting, sighing, now I bend my inclined head white.

Pavilion Night [(240)]

◎ *Du Fu*

Toward th' close of th' year, the sun and moon
Shorten the span of daylight high;
At the horizon, frost and snow
Reflect their sheen on th' chill night sky.
Fore th' peep of dawn, the horns and drums
Are sounding sad, heroic in air.
The Starry Stream as mirrored in
The Triple Gorges doth flutter and flare.
Thousands of families, mourning, wail
In th' wild for th' loss of their dear and young.
The woodcutters and fishermen
Of several parts, folk songs have sung.
The Lying Dragon, th' Galloping Horse,
Are all now buried neath the soil;
With my relations and tidings severed,
A shadow am I, a flimsy foil.

Ascending a Height

◎ *Du Fu*

Wind gusts blow fast, heaven's vault archeth high
And the gibbons screech sadly to cry;
The ait looketh clear, the sands spread white
And birds to and fro fly.
The boundless crop of autumnal leaves
Are rustling ceaselessly down;
The endless streams of the Long River
Are rolling forever on.
As a wanderer for ten thousand *li*
I mourn these days of late fall;
Arising on this terrace all alone,
I think of my sickly days livelong.
I hate these hard times increasing daily
My temple locks of frost hoar.
I have just renounced my stoup, sodden
With troubles and frailties sore.

A Song on Watching Lady Gongsun's Disciple in Her "Rapier Thrusting and Fencing" Dance

◎ *Du Fu*

Proem: On the 19th of the tenth moon in the second year of Dali[241], at the mansion-house of Yuanchi, the deputy sheriff of Kuizhou[242], I saw the sword dance of Li, the Twelfth Lady of Linying. Being struck by the magnificent spectacle, I asked her about the master of her art. She said, "I am Lady Gongsun's disciple." Early in the fifth year of Kaiyuan[243], I was still a child. Then, I remember, in the *xian* Yancheng, I had the hap to watch Gongsun's sword-pyrrhic dance, whirling, forceful and fraught with rhythmical grace, quite out of the common; from the two inner-court dancing troupes Yichun and Liyuan[244] to the outer-court one, among the *danseuses* and men-dancers conversant with this dance, during the early years of our Sage-artistic and Holy-militant Emperor[245], Gongsun was the sole select person. Reminiscent of her jade-like countenance and brocaded raiment, (I could not hope to see her again, while) I myself have become hoary-headed today; now even her disciple is no more like her then in the bloom of her youth. Tracing the source of my present spectacle, I see the mistress and her disciple are surprisingly equal in their impeccable arts. Dwelling feelingly on such footprints of time, I compose herewith the song below on this unforgettable event. In the past, Zhang Xu[246] of Wu, noted for his *cao* mode of calligraphy, having many a time observed in Ye *xian* Lady Gongsun perform the Xihe sword dance, became therefrom excelling in his calligraphic art. Since Zhang's mastery of his talents was due to the influence exerted on him by her dancing graces, the beauties of her art itself can readily be imagined.

There was a lady fair by the name of Gongsun,
Whose wondrous "Fencing" dance spread her fame far and near.
Her spectators crowded round like mountain crags,
Astounded all while heaven and earth hailed with cheer.
Like Yi[247] in a flash having nine suns shot down,
Like godheads driving dragons swiftly along,
She cometh like thunder-claps withdrawing their wrath,
And pauseth like streams and seas with their glory on.
Her red-lipped songs and pearl-sleeved dances mute and still,
Of late her disciple continueth her splendid grace.
The spirited Linying beauty from Baidi Town
Performeth this song with dance her mistress to trace.
In our exchange of words having learnt the source,
I dwell on past events thoughtful of each case.
Among the hundreds of court troupe artistes fair,
Gongsun's "Fencing" dance ranked certes the very first.
For fifty years as in turning over one's palm,
The vast sand storm[248] hast on the ruling house burst.
The court troupe members have all dispersed like smoke,
But one bright star still sparkleth in the cold air[249].
The mausoleum trees[250] have now grown tall;
In the stone-walled town[251] at Qutang the grasses are bare.
The strings and pipes with the song are ended and mute,
The rapture over as sadness bideth with the moon.
Being an aged man I know not where to wend,
As with foot corns and for tramping rocky paths
Of mountains wild, I grieve to leave too soon[252].

Ascending Yueyang Tower⁽²⁵³⁾

◎ *Du Fu*

Th' expanse of Dongting's waters⁽²⁵⁴⁾ long I've heard;
Today I ascend the Yueyang Tower to command.
The states Chu and Wu were here southeasterly split;
All heaven and earth by day and night seem its strand.
My kith and kin a single word send me not;
I feel both aged and ill on this sole boat.
Our border legions line up north of the Pass Mount⁽²⁵⁵⁾;
By the tower window, my tears stream forth as by rote.

Chancellor of Shu⁽²⁵⁶⁾

◎ *Du Fu*

The Memorial Hall of the Chancellor — where is its site to be found?
Beyond th' walls of Jinguan Town, a cedar old riseth there thickset and
    tall.
The fresh verdure of th' lawn reflecteth on the steps vernal hues by
    itself;
In the foliage chanteth in vain⁽²⁵⁷⁾ the golden oriole's tuneful call.
Being visited thrice and then oft times conferred on affairs of statecraft,
In installing and propping up two reigns as their adamantine support,
You in person the state's corps dispatch led, but died before triumph
    could be won:
It doth make all our heroes, for mourning your noble cause, to tears e'er
    resort.

Facing Snowing[258]

◎ *Du Fu*

Hosts of the ghosts of the fall'n in the battle are bewailed for;
Sadly doth sing all alone by himself an old wretched man.
Masses of the cloud bank are hanging low down o'er the rising dusk;
Rapidly drifted, the snow flakes are dancing and swirl as van.
Laid aside hath been my gourd shell and vacant my mug[259] remaineth;
Idle hath become the existing but sick stove as if in glow.
Several states are all severed in tidings[260] the meanwhile;
Sitting alone in lorn grief, I could but with "huh!" the air sow[261].

Thoughts During My Night Travel[262]

◎ *Du Fu*

Slim sedges are fluttered by a gentle breeze on the bank;
A mast ariseth sheer in my lone night barque.
The stars hang sparkling o'er the plain's broad expanse,
The moon is silvering the River's waves dark.
My name of note is not just to my letters[263] due.
Mine office relieved, for illness and old age dull.
To fluff now here, then there, what am I like?
'Twixt heaven and earth, a mere sandy beach gull.

Lines Written in the Desert

◎ *Cen Shen*[1]

Riding ever westwards as if for the sky,
Twice I saw the moon wax full all along.
I know not where I shall put up for the night;
Ever and aye the sands extend and extend on.

Night Mooring at Fengqiao Village

◎ *Zhang Ji*[2]

The moon is sinking; a crow croaks a-dreaming;
'Neath the night sky the frost casts a haze;
Few fishing-boat lights of th' riverside village
Are dozing off in their mutual sad gaze.
From the Cold Hill Bonzary outside
The city wall of Gusu town[3],
The resounding bell is tolling its clangour
At midnight to the passenger ship down.

---

[1] Cen Shen (715 – 770), a poet in the Tang Dynasty known for his frontier poems.
[2] Zhang Ji (715? – 779?), courtesy name Yisun, a Tang poet.
[3] Suzhou.

The Mountain Stream in the West of Chuzhou[①]

◎ *Wei Yingwu*[②]

Alone I fondly find rich meadow spread
On the bank of the mountain stream;
High up above an oriole is singing
In the tree's thick foliage;
Spring tide with rains flows fast before evening falls;
A boat alongside the ferry wild by itself lies.

---

① This poem is very beautiful. The defect, however, is that orioles never sing in the evening rains. The first two lines, therefore, are scarcely possible to form into one with the next two.
② Wei Yingwu (circa 737 – 789), nicknamed Wei Suzhou, a famous mid-Tang poet strongly influenced by the 5th-century poet Tao Yuanming.

Borderland Tunes

◎ *Lu Lun*[1]

(I)

In the forest dark the weeds by wild gusts were shocked;
The general[2] drew hard his mighty bow.
Early next morn the feathered arrow is found;
Stuck deep in a rock cleft on a boulder low.

(II)

The moon is hidden dark; the boreas roars.
The khan has fled windward in the night northwards.
We think of chasing him with a light mounted force;
Blinding snow falls all o'er our bows and swords.

---

[1] Lu Lun (circa 748 – 800), courtesy name Yunyan, a poet of the middle Tang Dynasty known for his frontier poems.

[2] The general alludes to Li Guang (李广), who served the three dynasties of Wen-*di* (文帝), Jing-*di* (景帝) and Wu-*di* (武帝) of the Han Dynasty. He was a terror to the Hun renowned for his mighty, accurate shooting.

The Wandering Son's Song

◎ *Meng Jiao*[1]

The thread from my dear mother's hand
Was sewn in the clothes of her wandering son.
For fear of my belated return,
Before my leave they were closely woven.
Who says mine heart like a blade of grass
Could repay her love's gentle beams of spring sun?

In the Capital's Southern Village

◎ *Cui Hu*[2]

On this same day last year within this door,
A comely face and peach blooms together did glow.
She I've admired has gone I know not where,
Th' peach blooms are smiling still in th' breeze to blow.

[1] Meng Jiao (751 – 814), courtesy name Dongye, a poet of the Tang Dynasty, noted for his portrayal of the harsh reality.

[2] Cui Hu (772 – 846), courtesy name Yingong, a poet of the Tang Dynasty, best known for the present quoted poem.

On the Rear Dhyana Hall of Po Shan Bonzary

◎ *Chang Jian*[1]

When at dawn I repaired to the bonzary old,
The first beams of the rising sun shone on trees tall.
Winding paths led to covert, secluded groves
Where lush thicket and flowers enclosed th' dhyana hall.
The rare aura of the mount pleased the nature of the birds,
Images in rock pit pools freed one's mind's ups and downs.
All the hubbubs of men were hushed as by a spell:
There was nothing left but the bell's and *qing*'s clangs.

Putting up at Wang Changling's Hermitage[2]

◎ *Chang Jian*

The limpid stream floweth unfathomably deep,
In solitary clouds is enshrouded the quiet hut.
Through the dense pine leafage peepeth down the shaded moon,
Whose crystalline beamings for thy pure sake illume.
By the bulrush-thatched arbour sleep the flower shadows,
In the court where peonies bloom deep green moss groweth thick.
In this vacant air, I too become released from the world,
Befriending phoenixes and storks of the western hills.

---

① Chang Jian (active in the early 8th century), an idyllic poet.
② The translator intended to touch up the English version of this poem, but had failed to do so because of his age and degenerating health. — Ed.

The Lay of the Stone Drums

◎ *Han Yu*[①]

With the inscription of the Stone Drums in his hand,
Sire Zhang urged me to make a song of them.
Du Fu is gone and the exiled faery[(264)] no more;
Being poor in gift, what could I do with the Drums?
The sceptre of Zhou sank low and chaos bore sway;
Xuan-wang[(265)] then arose to draw his heavenly sword.
He won and held court to receive homage and hurrah;
His vassals thronged, their sabers jostled and sang.
They gathered at Qiyang[(266)] to vie in splendour;
Games thousands of *li* around were hunted to repast.
Thus the feat was carved to tell all ages to come,
After stones were quarried from heights and these were hewn, —
Attendant courtiers, masters of letters and of art,
Were chosen to compose and brush the work, —
And thence ten blocks were left by the mountainside.
Rains drenched; the sun scorched and wild fire burned round them;
May spirits guard them all along from harm!
Where do you, Sire, get these paper rubbings from,
The gross and minutiae all here, full-formed and clear?
Bearing words strict and sense close, but hard to ken,
The type of character is not *li* nor *ke*[(267)].
Old in years, might not the script lose some strokes now?
There, water-dragons[(268)] and hog-dragons are slashed;

---

① Han Yu (768 – 824), courtesy name Tuizhi, a prominent writer, poet, and government official of the Tang Dynasty. Han Yu was an important Confucian intellectual who influenced later generations of Confucian thinkers, and led a reform in prose writing to return to a classical style that is simple, logical, and exact. He is considered one of China's finest prose writers.

Bright phoenixes hover round and faeries descend;
Green jade and coral trees intertwining grow;
Gold rope with cord of iron twist to a knot;
A bronze tripodal vessel jumps out of water ...
Ignored by ribald scholars in garnering poetry,
The two *yas* included not poems of stately size[269].
Confucius traveling westward entered not Qin[270],
In raising stars to the sky he missed Xi and E.
Too late, alas! was I born an antiquary,
For this I must let flow two streams of tears.
I recall when I first donned the doctor's robe,
That year our lord had his reign named Yuanhe[271];
A friend commanding troops right of Chang'an[272],
Had thought of digging for me the precious remains.
I washed my hat and bathed to tell those in power,
Such priceless treasure does not exist often.
In felt and mat they could be quickly wrapped,
Ten Drums may be laden on not many camels.
Compared with trophies[273], in the Temple Imperial,
Exceeds not the worth of these a hundredfold?
If our good lord let them be laid in the College,
What fruits could pupils under tuition then reap!
To see the show of classics at Hongdu[274],
The whole country did rush to throng the town.
When scraped of moss and lichen, showing their tendons,
These could be securely placed, even on the ground;
'Neath gable-roof deep and held in structure big,
They will pass through long ages without mishap.
High officials old in dealing with the world,
Not thankful at all, prefer to hesitate.
Thus, cowboys strike for fire, horns oxen sharpen;
Who'd touch and rub them ever with loving care?
They daily, monthly, weather-worn, in clay sunk,

For six years I looked to the west and sighed to naught.
The common brush-work charming of Xizhi
On a few sheets of paper could yet win him white geese[275].
When warfare for eight dynasties since Zhou stilled,
Why is it none cares to put these in goodly order?
Now peace has come to stay, nothing disturbs;
To the fore comes learning, revered are Qiu and Ke[276].
How could the reasons just named convince someone,
As to start an eloquent tongue flow river waves?
The Lay of the Stone Drums here draws to a close,
Alas! I fear time will be lost, but in vain.

An Eulogium on a Humble Cell

◎ *Liu Yuxi*[1]

A mount needs not be high; it becomes noted when on it fairies dwell.

A body of water needs not be deep; it would be ensouled, if a dragon makes it its resting whereabouts.

This hut of mine is a humble one, but I make it virtuously fragrant in repute.

The green moss creeping on the stepping stones and the verdure in the courtyard peeping through the screen do tell the presence of spring.

Here could be heard the table-talks and laughters of renowned scholars, but the rough and gross come not hither their wares to sell.

Here plain table-heptachord could be plucked and golden classics read the worldly cares to quell.

But there are without riotous strings and pipes to confuse the ears, and tedious official documents to ring quietude's knell.

Zhuge's recluse cottage at Nanyang and Yang Xiong's hermit arbour in West Shu, — according to Confucius, wherefore could either one of them be branded as a humble cell?

---

[1] Liu Yuxi (772 – 842), courtesy name Mengde, a poet, philosopher, and essayist of the Tang Dynasty. His poetry covers a wide range of subject matters and often follows a simple, "folk song" style.

Autumnal Song

◎ *Liu Yuxi*

Since of yore fall is grieved as lone and vacant,
Methinks autumnal days excel the spring morn.
A crane ascends through the clouds to the radiant sky,
Leading poetic thoughts to the boundless azure.

Bamboo Twig Song

◎ *Liu Yuxi*

Peach blooms on the mountain slopes in full flush blow,
The River's spring streams along the rocky banks flow.
The flowers pink would easily fade like thy love,
The endless currents would rush on like my sorrow.

Black Coat Lane⁽²⁷⁷⁾

◎ *Liu Yuxi*

Wild nameless flowers by the Cinnabar Bird Bridge
Are aglow in the last sun-beams in the Black Coat Lane.
The swallows 'fore the Wang and Xie noble mansions
Now fly into the nobodies' homestalls.

Stone-Walled City[(278)]

◎ *Liu Yuxi*

A chain of hills surrounds the capital old,
The tides the empty city beat and mutely ebb.
The old-time moon on the east side of the Huai Stream,
In the depth of night still crosses the low parapet.

Grasses

◎ *Bai Juyi*[①]

Tall and hanging down, the grasses on the wide plain
Flourish and wither once in every year.
Wild fire could not burn them up to extirpate;
Springtide zephyrs blow and they come to life again.
Distant verdure overcometh ancient highways;
Fair-day emerald stretcheth away to waste cities.
Bidding farewell to wanderers going somewhither,
Lush-growing grasses waft in the breeze full of parting cares.

---

① Bai Juyi (772 – 846), courtesy name Letian and style name Xiangshan Resident, a renowned poet and government official of the Tang Dynasty. Bai Juyi has been known for his plain, direct, and easily comprehensible style of verse, as well as for his social and political criticism.

On Sighting the Mounts with the Bonze Haochu, Lines Written to My Kin and Friends in the Capital

◎ *Liu Zongyuan*[1]

Shrill, seaside peaks like poniards pointing skywards
In this fall day everywhere my sad bowels pierce.
How could I be turned into a million selves
To be scattered on to those tops to descry my homeland?

Abiding by the Runlet[(279)]

◎ *Liu Zongyuan*

For long being entangled by ties of office,
I sense fine hap as an exile to the wild South.
In my leisurely sojourn with farming neighbours,
I feel I am somewhat like a mountain sylvan.
In daybreak tillage upturning dewy weeds,
In nightly row resounding oar strokes from bank rocks,
I come and go without meeting anyone,
And sing aloud 'neath the azure sky of Chu.

---

[1] Liu Zongyuan (773 – 819), courtesy name Zihou, a prominent writer, poet, and government official of the Tang Dynasty. Along with Han Yu, he led the Classical Prose Movement. His prose is characterized by sagacity and poignancy.

Snowing on the River[(280)]

◎ *Liu Zongyuan*

Not a bird o'er the hundreds of peaks,
Not a man on the thousands of trails.
An old angler alone in a boat,
With his rod and line, in raining outfit,
Is fishing on the river midst th' snowdrift.

The Angler[①]

◎ *Liu Zongyuan*

The angler passing his night by the West Mount,
Some limpid water from the Xiang Stream drawn,
Doth kindle bamboo stems verdant to heat at dawn,
The smoke being dispersed the sun arising,
He is seen not; the scull "*ai-nai*" doth sound, —
A green expanse show the water and the mount;
A skiff from above descendeth down the midstream;
About the crags the carefree clouds rush round.

---

① From the original 楚竹 (bamboos of Chu), we know this poem was written during the poet's exile to Yongzhou (永州).

A Call on the Recluse Who Is Just Out

◎ *Jia Dao*[1]

I asked the boy beneath the pine tree,
Who said, "The master's gone herbs to pick;
He must be somewhere around these clifts,
Concealed unseen in the clouds thick."

Jiling Terrace[(281)]

◎ *Zhang Hu*[2]

The fair State Queen of Guo, in favour supreme,
At full ope dawn doth ride in the palace gate;
For disliking rouge and powder to daub her beauty,
She leaveth her eyebrows light, to tend on the potentate.

---

[1] Jia Dao (779 – 843), courtesy name Langxian, a poet known for his assiduity in composing poems.
[2] Zhang Hu (circa 785 – 852), courtesy name Chengji, a poet who did not like Confucian classics and lived in seclusion throughout his life, visiting scenic places and Buddhist temples.

Mountain Trip

◎ *Du Mu*[1]

Far up the mountainside the stone trail wound,
Where the clouds were thick, there stood some abodes.
I stopt my cart to watch the maple forest late
With frost-bitten leaves more crimson than spring blooms.

Lines in Bidding Adieu

◎ *Du Mu*

Moved with lorn cares yet appearing placid,
We feel not like changing smiles at our stoups,
But the candle is thoughtful of our parting,
Shedding tears all night long till the peep of dawn.

---

[1] Du Mu (803 – 852), courtesy name Muzhi, a leading poet of the late Tang Dynasty, best known for his lyrical and romantic quatrains featuring historical sites or romantic situations.

The Clear-and-Bright Feast⁽²⁸²⁾

◎ *Du Mu*

Upon the Clear-and-Bright Feast of spring
The rain drizzleth down in spray.
Pedestrians on countryside ways
In gloom are pining away.
When asked "Where a tavern fair for rest
Is hereabouts to be found,"
The shepherd boy the Apricot Bloom Vill
Doth point to afar and say.

Hearing Tartar Clarinet on the Border

◎ *Du Mu*

Whence is blown the clarinet at sunset?
Border mountain parapets 'neath a high bird
Hideth wolf dung smoke columns from one's sight.
Visitors hearing it would have their hair turned white.
For nineteen years all along, Su Wu had this heard!

Plaints from the Gemmed Harp[283]

◎ *Wen Tingyun*[1]

On the cool mat of woven bamboo strips,
In a silver framed bed, dreamless I lie.
The azure sky is like flooding water
And the clouds of night float lightly in the sky.
The cries of wild geese sound afar
Toward the Xiao and Xiang Streams' valleys.
In the Twelve Storeyed Houses of the faerie land[284]
The moon shineth brightly (o'er the galleries).

The Gladdening Upland[285]

◎ *Li Shangyin*[2]

Toward eve, troubled I feel,
So drive my cart to the Old Plain.
How wondrous looks the sundown!
What a pity 'tis nearing dusk.

---

[1] Wen Tingyun (812 – 870), courtesy name Feiqing, an important lyricist of the late Tang Dynasty. Most of his poems are "boudoir" verses describing solitary women and their hidden desires.
[2] Li Shangyin (813 – 858), an important poet of the late Tang Dynasty. He is particularly famous for his cryptic "no title" poems. The numerous allusions in his poems make translation extremely difficult.

Lines Sent to the North Written During Night Rains⁽²⁸⁶⁾

◎ *Li Shangyin*

Being asked for my home-coming date,
I tell thee I'm not sure when that'll be,
As night rains on the mounts of Ba fall
And autumn pools are brimmed from the lea.
Then we shall by the west window sit,
Clipping the candle wick in some night,
And talk of the night rains on th' Ba mounts,
When I think of thee with mute delight.

Chang'e⁽²⁸⁷⁾

◎ *Li Shangyin*

High mica screens illumed in flashes
By flickering lights of candles tall;
The Silvery Stream^① beginning to fade
And the Morning Star to fall.
Chang'e should now sorely regret
For stealing the herb of fay,
So she hath to face all alone the blue sky
And the sea immense night and day.

① The Milky Way.

Villages Deserted after the March of Troops

◎ *Han Wo*[1]

The streams still flush and the sun still slants,
All cocks and dogs are mute, but still croak the crows.
All the villages seem to keep the Cold Repast;[(288)]
No people could be seen, but merely flowers.

---

[1] Han Wo (circa 842 – 923), courtesy name Zhiyao or Zhiguang, a poet of the late Tang Dynasty and a witness of its downfall.

Notes and Comments

(1) *Liang County Song* is the text for singing the *Liang County Tune* in the *Garner of Tunes*（《乐府》）of the Tang Dynasty. Liangzhou is, nowadays, Wuwei county, Gansu Province. The character "仞" represents a linear measure unit in ancient China of 7 ancient Chinese feet long. The Qiang flute was a wind instrument of one of the minorities outside of the northwest regions of ancient China, later on often played in the military band. The "杨柳" (willow) refers to an ancient song named "Plucking Willows". The original locality of the Jade Gate Pass lies in the northwest of Dunhuang county, Gansu Province. The last two lines say that "Why does someone have to play the 'Plucking Willows' on the Qiang flute with its sullen note to complain of the latecoming of spring? People should learn that spring breeze would never reach farther on than the Jade Gate Pass." Between the lines, the lack of concern on the part of the imperial court for the frontier guards is insinuated.

(2) The *bi-li* (written in Chinese as 觱篥, 筚篥 or 悲篥) pipe originated from Qiuci（龟兹）, one of the thirty-six states of West Land（西域）, now mainly lying in China's Xinjiang Uygur Autonomous Region, whither Emperor Wu-di of Han（汉武帝）sent his great general Zhang Qian（张骞）in 139 BC as ambassador extraordinary to establish diplomatic relations and economic and cultural communications.

(3) It was commonly believed in ancient Cathay that a dragon's groaning would cause springs to bubble forth and a roaring tiger would provoke the winds blowing.

(4) The original《渔阳掺》, also called《渔阳参挝》, was a drum tune stricken by the youthful and highly gifted scholar and poet Mi Heng（祢衡）of East Han（东汉）at a feast to which a great company of court officials were invited by Cao Cao（曹操）, the chancellor. Mi was ordered by Cao to beat on a big drum to amuse his guests, which was as well an insult to the young scholar for his arrogant attitude towards the overpowering courtier. Mi accepted the challenge and hit back by first undressing his gown and upper garment, then beating on the big drum a furiously rapid tune as a defiant protest to Cao and finally putting on his clothes to go away. According to Yu Xin's（庾信, fl. 540–560）poem *Listening to the Clubbing of Laundered Clothes at Night*（《夜听捣衣诗》）, a line "Rapid clubbings sound like Yuyang drum beats"（杵急渔阳掺）gives an inkling of the nature of this drum tune.

(5) The original "Willows" (杨柳) signifies the ancient song *Picking Willow Twigs* (《折杨柳枝》) turning to a light, breezy new tune.

(6) Ehuang (娥皇) and Nüying (女英) were the two princesses of *Di* Yao (帝尧, fabled to have reigned from 2357 to 2257 BC) of Taotang (陶唐), given by him in marriage to Shun of Yu (虞舜, 2255–2207 BC), also named Zhonghua (重华), as his dual spouses. Legendary lore has it that *Di* Shun (帝舜) died in the wilds of Cangwu (苍梧之野) while leading his expedition against the rebellious Miao (苗) tribesmen. On hearing the tidings of his unexpected illness, they sped southward trying to succour him. But when they got to the Limpid Xiang Stream (潇湘), a furious squall overtook them and they were drowned without being able to catch sight of their dear lord, alive or dead. In Qu Yuan's (屈原, 345–286 BC) great self-mourning ode *Hailing Home the Soul* (《招魂》), the last line says:

"魂兮归来哀江南！"

（Come back, oh my soul, to the south of Stream Ai!）

"'Ai' in the original means 'sorrow.' Stream Sorrow (哀江) is the section of Xiang Stream (湘水) called Limpid Xiang confluent with Miluo River (汨罗江), flowing northward into the Dongting Lake (洞庭湖). It has two islets called Great Sorrow and Small Sorrow (大小哀洲). Legend has it that Shun's two queens following in pursuit of, but failing to catch up with, him in his southern campaign, cried bitterly on these two islets, hence their names." — quoted from § 19 of VII, *Chü Yuan and His Works*, Introduction to *Poetry III*.

This renowned poem of Li Bai in the manner of *Garner of Tunes* poems of Han and Wei (汉、魏《乐府》诗), with irregular measures and rhymings like the Pindaric odes, makes use of the final, long departure of Shun from his dear queens, Yao's two princesses Ehuang and Nüying, as a tragic setting for the poet's feelings of alarm, indignation, sorrow and helplessness over the political mess made by Emperor Xuan-*zong* in his dotage. The theme and feelings are allusively and tersely, as well as discreetly and vaguely hinted at, to avoid wrathful persecution or fatal revenge from those the poet would certainly offend. *The Lay of the Sun Arising and Sinking* in the like vein and of the like matter is more hazy.

(7) The previous lines speak of Ehuang and Nüying's doomed departing from their lord as tragic. Here, it is insinuated that the court debaucheries ("Wanton waves," see note to *The Lay of the Sun Arising and Sinking*) and Xuan-*zong*'s blind trust of state affairs in Li Linfu and Yang Guozhong and that of military authority in An Lushan are bound for tragic and fatal outcome: the poet's

counsel to the country would be of no avail.

(8) "I do fear Providence would not decree matters as I, cherishing my fidelity to the Emperor, wish things to happen."

(9) According to *The Chronicle of Bamboo Strips* (《竹书纪年》), unearthed from King Xiang of Wei's (魏襄王) mausoleum in the second year of the Taikang Period of Wu-*di* of Jin (晋武帝太康二年，281) plundered by a Ji County (汲郡) subject called Bu Zhun (不准) in several tens of cart loads, *Di* Yao when advanced in age was banished to Pingyang (平阳) and imprisoned by Shun. This is contrary to *Di* Yao and *Di* Shun's traditionally good names and relations. To say Yao and Shun would have to abdicate to give place to Yu is simply an exaggeration to bring forth and foreshadow the following thoughts.

(10) These four lines may allude to Xuan-*zong*'s entrusting of power in Li Linfu, Yang Guozhong, An Lushan and Geshu Han or these five and the next lines may allude to his prince Su-*zong*'s (肃宗) coronation as emperor at Lingwu (灵武) and the latter's eunuch Li Fuguo (李辅国) faking his imperial decree to enforce the removal of Xuan-*zong*'s living quarters to the western part of the palace. Soon after this compulsory removal, Xuan-*zong* died of anger and grief.

(11) *Di* Shun was known to be duo-pupiled.

(12) There is a species of bamboo with sparse spots of mauve, traditionally said to be the tear stains of Ehuang and Nüying. Legendary lore has it that before the two sisters were drowned, they wailed bitterly facing the Plain of Cangwu; their tears sprinkled on the bamboo poles kept fast and lasted forever.

(13) Cancong and Yufu were ancient legendary kings who founded the state Shu over forty millennia ago. It was isolated from the Middle Empire till its conquest by King Hui of Qin (秦惠王) in 316 BC.

(14) Noble White Alp (太白山) lay in the west of the then capital Chang'an (长安) of the Tang Dynasty (唐朝), as it still does so in the west of the provincial chief city Xi'an (西安) of Shaanxi Province (陕西省) today. It was and is capped with snow all the year round, hence its name.

(15) It was said that King Hui of Qin sent five beautiful maidens to marry five princes of Shu. Shu dispatched five envoys of giant strength to greet the brides. On their way back to Zitong (梓潼), they came across a huge serpent entering its recess. They pulled its tail to drag it out. As a result the mountain crumbled, the five envoys were all crashed to death and the five beauties rose to a mountaintop that was not undermined and were gorgonized.

(16) Xihe (羲和) is said to drive the chariot drawn by six dragons in which the

God of Sun rides. When he drives to the highest cliff, he has to turn round his chariot to wind his way about.

(17) Yellow storks are said to be of the highest flight.

(18) The Blue Sod Alps (青泥岭), in Lüeyang *xian* (略阳县), Shaanxi Province at present, is noted for its "twist and turn in winding about."

(19) Shu is in the southwest of Qin (秦).

(20) The cuckoos (子规、杜宇、杜鹃、望帝) are sad in their cries. One of the legends has it that Wang-*di*, the King of Shu, raped his premier's wife, felt ashamed of himself and escaped to turn himself into a bird sadly crying his own name to show regret.

(21) The Sword Steeple (剑阁) is between the Great Sword Mountain and the Small Sword Mountain in the northeast of the Sword Steeple *xian* of Sichuan Province today. It is the main passage or pass between Sichuan and Shaanxi Provinces, a part of the Southern Flight of Steps (南栈道).

(22) *Crows Croaking at Dusk* (《乌夜啼》) is an old traditional theme and title in *The Garner of Tunes* poems. It was said to be first written by a certain Wang Yiqing (王义庆) during the Yuanjia (元嘉) years (424–453) of the dynasty Liu Song (刘宋, 420–479). In *The Garner of Tunes Anthology* (《乐府诗集》), there are eight poems so entitled. In the *Lives of Noted Women* (《列女传》) of the *Jin Dynasty Chronicle* (《晋书》), Dou Tao's (窦滔) wife Su Hui (苏蕙), when her husband was exiled to Liu Sha (流沙) by his king Fu Jian (符坚) of Fore Qin (前秦), wove a series of palindromic and rondure poems on a broad piece of silk taffeta (织锦为《迴文旋图诗》) and sent it to him to show her commiserating love and devotion. It has been said that Li Bai probably used this traditional theme and title to voice his critical dissent from Emperor Xuan-*zong*'s border expansion policy.

(23) The palindromic and rondure poem (回文诗, 璇玑图) was ingeniously composed and then woven into such a pattern in a piece of taffeta that a host of variant versions of it could be read from the top down regularly to the end as well as from the end up reversely to the top and crosswise from the right to the left and then also from the left to the right in a number of roundabout ways. As the Chinese language consists of characters (in their written form, made up of strokes) each having a sound and a meaning of its own, unlike the western, Indo-European languages, which are all composed of words formed by combining alphabets to shape syllables and joining syllables to make words or particles, so it is possible in Chinese to join up two to three, four, five, six, seven or even eight characters to make a phrase, clause, sentence or line of verse. In Su Hui's original palindromic and rondure

poem, which is composed of 840 characters, woven in a piece of taffeta said to be 8 inches square, a Buddhist bonze by the name of Qi-*zong* (起宗) living at the turning of the Song (宋, 960–1279) to the Yuan (元，1206–1368) Dynasties, found out 3,752 poems of 3-charactered, 4-charactered, 5-charactered, 6-charactered and 7-charactered in these 840 characters. And a certain Kang Wanmin (康万民) of the Ming Dynasty (1368–1644) added another "Xuanji" picture (璇玑图) and read out 4,206 poems from Su Hui's original poem.

(24) Gusu Terrace (姑苏台) is on Gusu Mount (姑苏山), a range of hillocks thirty *li* southwest of the present Suzhou City (苏州市), which was anciently called Gusu. The Terrace, also known as Xu Terrace (胥台), was first built by Fuchai's father King Helü of Wu (吴王阖闾). Fuchai expanded the Terrace and spent three years to build the Spring Night Palace (春宵宫) for whole night carousals. Fuchai's prince royal You (友) burnt down the palace when his defending troops were completely crushed by Goujian's invading legions.

(25) Fuchai (夫差, ?–473 BC), King of the state Wu (吴) at the end of the Spring and Autumn Period (春秋, 770–476 BC) of the Zhou Dynasty (周, 1046–256 BC), overcame the armed forces of the state Yue (越) with a thrashing defeat and pierced into its capital Guiji (会稽). Goujian (勾践, ?–465 BC), king of Yue, sued for peace, bribed Wu's chief courtier Pi (太宰嚭) and knew his enemy to be fond of women, sent two exquisite beauties, Xishi (西施) and Zheng Dan (郑旦), as human tributes of indemnity to pacify the victor. After twenty years of recuperation and incessant strengthening, Goujian, taking advantage of his enemy's haughtiness and conceit, and leading all his hardened troops in person far away from the capital to attend a gathering of friendly state heads, forced a swift, resolute campaign to crush Wu and took over the control of its capital completely. Fuchai committed suicide and Wu was annexed by Yue. Such is the political background of this poem.

This poem was not just a memorial lyric of historical events, according to the critic Zhan Ying (詹锳): It was an occult warning by our poet to his emperor Xuan-*zong* of Tang whose imperial concubine bore resemblance to Xishi in beauty as well as in the circumstances of her monarch's dotingness on her — Fuchai lost his state and his life on account of Xishi, so Xuan-*zong* was going to lose his for Yang Yuhuan (杨玉环). Confer the notes on *The Lay of the Sun Arising and Sinking*.

(26) This was the copper-cased water-dripping timepiece, the clepsydra (铜壶

滴漏，漏壶），with a silverpin (attached to a bamboo float to buoy it up) to indicate how much water had dripped for showing the passage of time, before the introduction of clocks and watches during the Ming Dynasty from Europe.

(27) According to *Huainan-zi* （《淮南子》），a work of legendary lore and metaphysical strivings of the Lao-*zi* （老子）School of thought by Liu An （刘安，179–122 BC），the Sun rides a radiant chariot drawn by six flaming dragons.

(28) The driver of this solar chariot is Xihe （羲和）.

(29) The original of this line 羲和，羲和，汝奚汩没於荒淫之波 is taken by me to allude to Emperor Xuan-*zong*'s being completely submerged in his enslaving infatuation for Yang Taizhen （杨太真），his undue trust of imperial affairs, political and military, in his malignant chancellor Li Linfu （李林甫），her three cousins, especially Yang Guozhong （杨国忠），her three brothers-in-law and his Hu general An Lushan （安禄山）. The solar chariot at the time being driven by Xuan-*zong* is the Tang Dynasty in Li Bai's imaginative, metaphorical vista, and the Sun signifies *huang-di*, imperial or regal powers of all time. Yang Taizhen, the imperial concubine, was originally Prince Li Mao's （李瑁）wife and Xuan-*zong*'s daughter-in-law. After the decease of Xuan-*zong*'s favourite concubine Wu Hui-*fei* （武惠妃），Yang Taizhen was first ordained as a Taoist priestess to deceive the court's sense of decorum and then, in the fourth year of Tianbao （天宝四年，746），she was ceremonially appointed as his formal Imperial Concubine. Xuan-*zong* kept promiscuous relations with all her three sisters and she held similar secret affairs with her cousin Yang Guozhong and the Hu satrap general An Lushan, openly known as her foster son. Scholars and commentators have been silent during these thousand and two hundred odd years on these points which are the hidden meaning of Xihe being "sunk in the expanse of wanton waves." In the 14th year of Tianbao （天宝十四年，755），the military governor An Lushan, with his subordinate general Shi Siming （史思明），rebelled on account of the mutual jealousy between him and Yang Guozhong in their grasp for power and sexual promiscuities with Yang Taizhen. Luoyang （洛阳）and the then capital Chang'an fell to the foster son of the imperial concubine. Xuan-*zong* had to flee for his life to Shu before the fall of the capital; on his way of flight, he could not help having her strangled with a silk scarf and her cousin and paramour Yang Guozhong beheaded, to pacify the commanders of the imperial guard at the Mawei Post Station （马嵬驿）.

(30) According to *Huainan-zi*, Duke Luyang （鲁阳公）shook his lance at the sun

when he was engaged in close fighting with the chief of Han (韩) as the sun was going to set; immediately, the setting sun bounced back from the northwestern horizon for a distance of three *she* (三舍，ninety *li*), so that he could beat his antagonist in time. These four lines about monstrous Luyang's waving his lance at the sun seem to allude to An Lushan, Shi Siming and their fierce, marauding troops.

(31) An Lushan and Shi Siming's Hu (胡) troops were notorious for their cruelty, massacre and ravage of civilians of Luoyang, Chang'an, the capital, and thirteen counties of Jizhou (冀州), at present in Hebei Province (河北省). The rebellion lasted for more than seven years and was exhausted by patricides and murders in the rebels' own camps; it petered out with the suicide of Shi Siming's son in the first year of the Guangde Period (广德元年，763) of Dai-*zong* (代宗), the grandson of Xuan-*zong*. Our poet died in the previous year; so too did Xuan-*zong*, Li Bai's sovereign, and Su-*zong* (肃宗), Xuan-*zong*'s successor and Dai-*zong*'s father.

(32) The last two lines of the original seem to mean the poet bearing all the calamities of Xuan-*zong*'s reign with gloomy, distressing but patient resignation.

(33) Peonies were in glorious bloom in the imperial garden as the Emperor was enjoying their sight and fragrance, being attended by his doted concubine for the occasion. Ming Huang (明皇，formally known as Xuan-*zong* of Tang), sitting in the aloeswood arbour and touched with winsome fancies musical and poetic, wished Li Bai to compose poems for accompanying the new tunes of melody. He said, "Enjoying these renowned flowers while facing my concubine, why should we resort to old tunes?" When the poet was summoned to appear opportunely for composing new verses, he was already quite drunk. Court attendants splashed water on his face and handed him his writing brush. Li Guinian (李龟年), the court tunes-composer, -singer and -performer, handed the gold-speckled silk scroll to Li Bai. Instantly, he composed three quatrains of exquisite beauty and brushed them on the spread sheet (the stanza above being the first of them), members of the Court Singers and Players performed on strings and bamboo tubes, Li Guinian sang in accord and His Majesty attuned with a gem flute. Meanwhile, Yang Taizhen drank the West Liang (西凉) rare delicious port from a crystal chalice, wishing joy and longevity to her lord forever and aye.

— Taken from *Notable Happenings about Tang Poetry* (《唐诗纪事》) by Ji Yougong (计有功) of Song.

(34) The spray of wood-stemmed peony with its pink flowers sprinkled with dews is compared to Yang Taizhen, the imperial concubine graced with the Emperor's favours.

(35) The daughter of the Wu Mountains (巫山女神), as sung by Song Yu (宋玉) in his *A Fu on Gaotang* (《高唐赋》): "While leaving she said, 'I am in the south of the Wu Mountains and on the pinnacle rock of the highland; at dawn I am the morning clouds and towards sunset I become the showering rain; be it after daybreak or be it before dusk, I am always there below the southern elevation.'" The favours and love bestowed on the daughter of the Wu Mountains by King Huai of Chu (楚怀王) were but a legendary tale, not to be compared to the grace and affection of Xuan-*zong* given to her.

(36) Zhao Feiyan (赵飞燕), whose name means "The Flitting Swallow," was at first a maid of honour of Emperor Cheng of Han's (汉成帝) princess Yang'e (阳阿公主). She was a beauty and a light-footed dancer; deeply beloved by the monarch, she was formally married as his empress. Years later, after the emperor's decease, she was debased as a common female subject for her sexual misdemeanour, whereupon she committed suicide.

As Xuan-*zong* and his imperial concubine were enjoying the flowering peonies in the aloeswood arbour, our poet, as a member of the Court School of Literati (供奉翰林), was summoned to the feast and ordered to write poems for the occasion. He became part drunk and, having asked the attending chief eunuch Gao Lishi (高力士) to pull off his black silk high-heeled and thick-soled boots (靴), composed these three beautiful quatrains. The highly favoured eunuch resented the indignity and hit back by back-biting Li Bai as insinuating insults to the imperial concubine in his comparison of her to the Flitting Swallow and the daughter of the Wu Mountains. Our poet thus won the anger of the imperial concubine and the displeasure of the emperor.

(37) The climate of ancient Yan (燕), where the supposed poetess' husband is draughted for the armed forces, in the northern region of Hebei Province and the southwest of Liaoning Province today, is much colder than that of ancient Qin (秦) in Shaanxi Province today, where the supposed poetess is. So, when the grasses of Yan begin to turn verdant like tufts of green silk, the mulberry leaves of Qin are already thick and hanging low on the branches. When the husband is touched by the approach of spring as he sees the grasses turning green, the wife has for more days been struck by the mulberry leaves growing thick and hanging low on the branches of the trees. The dear wife is so devoted to her beloved husband that she does not wish the spring breeze,

a total stranger, to be wafted into her silk curtain piece.

(38) See note (37).

(39) This poem was supposed by the poet to be written by a Jin Dynasty (晋, 265–420) dame of the state Wu (吴国) called Ziye thinking of her enlisted husband. Chang'an was the capital of the Tang Dynasty. Gem Gateway or Gem Pass was one of the two ancient Passes, the other being called Yang Pass (阳关), the passage between the Tang Empire and West Domain (西域). It is in the west of Dunhuang *xian* (敦煌县) in Gansu Province (甘肃省) today.

(40) *Long Drawn Yearning* (《长相思》) is the title of one of the songs of *The Garner of Tunes* (《乐府》), which was originally named when the official organ was decreed to be set up by the emperor Wu-*di* of Han (汉武帝, 140–86 BC), after the device of the suburb sacrificial rites in paying homage to Heaven and Earth, as the imperial institute for collecting folk songs and composing tunes for musical accompaniment ("武帝定郊祀之礼，乃立乐府"). The song was the very first one of the twenty-five songs of ancient plaints (《长相思》古怨思二十五曲之一), derived from a very ancient poem "Up above, long drawn yearning is said; down below, long drawn parting is quothed" ("本古诗'上言长相思，下言久别离'"). In old songs, therefore, this short snatch "long drawn yearning" is often made use of for playing on dear rememberance. Li Bai also performs his tune on this age-long theme after the poets of Liang (梁) and Chen (陈) of the Six Dynasties (六朝).

(41) "The Beauteous One" in this imagined song of the supposed lady is meant by her to be her beloved mate.

(42) In the hallucination of the supposed poetess, her "Beauteous One" is seen by her at the horizon "vaulted above by the empyrean azure" and "by the expanse of clear waves upborne below."

(43) "The sky and earth where he is are thus far away that striving so hard as my soul doth, it cannot hope to reach there as the Mountain of the Gem Gateway Pass (玉门关) — that is, the Border Defile Mount — is thousands of *li* away from me." The Gem Gateway Pass, so renowned in the Tang poetry, in the county Dunhuang (敦煌) of Gansu Province today, was, according to Prince Zhanghuai (章怀太子), 3,600 *li* from the imperial capital Chang'an.

(44) Sand pyrus (沙棠) was said to be a highly buoyant wood growing on the Kunlun Mountains (昆仑山), the fruits of which when eaten by men would proof them against being drowned.

(45) These four lines in the original, rendered into eight in the English version, occasion difficulties to a critic Zhu Jian (朱谏), who says they are irrelevant

to their context as well as to themselves one another, and so the poem, he thinks, was probably composed by someone else who was, however, not a trifling poetaster, though not such an illustrious poet as Li Bai. A later critic Mei Dingzuo (梅鼎祚) dismisses this comment as a gross mistake. Wang Qi (王琦), the editor of the early Qianlong (乾隆) edition (1758) of Li Bai's *Complete Works*, opines that, the first two lines mean to say that to be intent upon becoming a fairy, one would not inevitably succeed in winning metamorphosis to fly heavenward, but to be free from wiles, forget one's identity and hive in consciousness with the gulls in their flights, one may attain spiritual freedom at the moment, while the next two lines mean to say that, to be intent upon poetic composition, one might in the end achieve immortal poetry such as Qu Yuan's, but to devote one's efforts to the establishment of worldly sights and visual glory such as the Chu (楚) kings' terraces and arbours, one could gain only transient satisfaction of the senses. The comparisons and contrasts between the first two instances and the second two would naturally give one the right choices. In short, the first two lines are related to the entertainment on the pyrus barge, while the second two are concerned with the lines following.

(46) To the west of ancient Ezhou (鄂州), called Wuchang (武昌) today, on the Yellow Crane Ait (黄鹄矶) in the Long River (长江) or Yangzi-*jiang* (扬子江), there stands the Yellow Crane Tower (黄鹤楼). The structure, first built in the second year of the Huangwu Period (黄武二年, 223) of Wu (吴), one of the Three Kingdoms (三国, 220–280), was burnt down and rebuilt many times through the centuries. It derives its name from one of the three or all these legendary anecdotes: ① Fei Hui (费祎, ? – 253), the Grand General (大将军) of Han of Shu (蜀汉), after his metamorphosis into a fairy, once rode back in flying astride a yellow crane to rest for a while on the Tower; ② According to *The Tales of Strange Events* (《述异记》) by Zu Chongzhi (祖冲之, 429 – 500, the great scientist of the South Dynasty, 南朝, 420 – 479), Xun Gui (荀瓌), once taking a rest on the Yellow Crane Tower in his trip to the east, noticed specks of something falling down in the southwestern horizon and before long, they came as riders of yellow cranes and alighted by the Tower; the cranes stopped at the entrance and their riders shared a feast indoors; soon after their entertainment, they rode off astride the cranes and disappeared; ③ According to *Reliques of South Qi* (《南齐志》) now lost, quoted by *Geographical Scenic Spots of Notability* (《舆地纪胜》) it is said that the fairy Wang Zi'an (王子安) often passed the Tower in his flights astride a yellow crane.

(47) The chapter *Luteous Emperor* of *Lie-zi*（《列子·黄帝》）speaks of a seaboard farer who kept close company with the seagulls daily. The birds, not afraid of him, often flew near him and even stopped to perch on his shoulders and arms. One day, his father said to him that he heard the birds were very familiar with him and so asked him to take one or two home to show them to himself. The next day when he went to the seaside, the gulls refrained from flying near him or stopping at his side.

(48) Qu Yuan（屈原）, the greatest as well as the earliest renowned poet of ancient Cathay (and the greatest statesman and patriot of his time to boot), whose formal names are Ping（平）and Zhengze（正则）, was a member of an anciently descended illustrious house closely related to the ruling royal family of the state Chu. His great ode *Lee Sao*（《离骚》— *Suffering Throes*）, *Nine Hymns*（《九歌》）, *A Sylva of Nine Pieces*（《九章》）, *Sky-Vaulting Queries*（《天问》）, *Distant Wanderings*（《远游》）and *Hailing Home the Soul*（《招魂》）are the few extant works known to have descended to us from some twenty-three centuries ago.

(49) Wang Qi, the editor of the Qianlong edition of *Li Bai's Complete Works*, mentions two such terraces, the Zhanghua Terrace（章华台）said to be located in Jianli *xian*（监利县）of Hubei Province today, and the Yunyang Terrace（云阳台）, in the Yunyang County（云阳邑）of the state Chu, now in Danyang *xian*（丹阳县）of Jiangsu Province. They are probably non-existent now, or at most in ruins.

(50) Xie Tiao（谢朓, 460? – 496?）, known also by his name of daily use Xuan Hui（玄晖）, an eminent poet of South Qi（南齐，479 – 502）of the Six Dynasties, has a poem *Ascending the Three-Peaked Mount before Dusk and Looking Back at the Capital*（《晚登三山还望京邑》）, with the lines:

> Sunset clouds spread into taffeta,
> The limpid River is like white tiffany.
> （馀云散成绮，澄江净如练。）

(51) Two mounts facing each other like the antennae of a silkworm's moth in the remote distance are thus called Emei（蛾眉）; so the range of mountains is also called Emei（峨眉）, written differently but pronounced the same, meaning the antennae of a silkworm's moth. The Buddhists called them the Luminous Mounts（光明山）, while the Taoists named them the Empty Spiritualized Hollowed Heaven（虚灵洞天）. The range is today in the southwest of Emei *xian*（峨眉县）of Sichuan Province. It is a branch of the Min Mountains（岷山）, rolling southward to the *xian* region and protruding in three mount peaks, called the Great *E*, the Middle *E* and the Small *E*（大

峨、中峨和小峨）.

(52) Pingqiang（平羌）, a stream, is also called Qingyi Stream（青衣水）, in the east of Emei.

(53) The original 青溪 means the Qingyi Stream.

(54) The Three Gorges: those of the Long River（长江）, Qutang（瞿塘）, Wu（巫）and Xiling（西陵）, being narrow passages of the stream between high mountains on both banks.

(55) Yuzhou's（渝州）ancient domain is now the city of Chongqing.

(56) Mount Lu（庐山）is in the south of the city Jiujiang（九江）, Jiangxi Province today. According to legendary lore, during the reign of King Wu of Zhou（周武王, 1046–1042 BC）, there were seven brothers of the family Kuang（匡）thatching their cottages on the side of this mountain and hence it has been called Mount Kuang or Kuang Lu (Lu meaning "cottages").

(57) Lu Xuzhou（卢虚舟, the poet's friend to whom this poem was addressed）, was Lord Attendant taking charge of insignia at court, Chief of the Guards and Security Warden of the Capital（殿中侍御史，掌殿廷仪卫及京城纠察）.

(58) According to the *Analects of Confucius*（《论语》）, "The lunatic of Chu Jieyu（楚狂接舆）sang his song when he walked passing Confucius: 'Phoenix, ah, Phoenix, how low hath virtue of the times sunk（凤兮凤兮，何德之衰）!'" And according to Huangfu Mi's（皇甫谧）*Lives of Men of High Virtues*（《高士传》）, Lu Tong（陆通）, called also with his common, daily appellative Jieyu（接舆）, a subject of the state Chu, seeing the chaotic state of affairs in politics during the reign of King Zhao of Chu（楚昭王）, affected to be a lunatic and declined to assume any office in the officialdom of his time. He counseled Confucius not to officiate for avoiding personal calamity.

(59) Here our poet, calling himself "the lunatic of Chu", compares his friend Lu Xuzhou to Confucius, by counselling him not to stay in office any longer, but to renounce the world and go with himself to visit the Five Renowned Mounts, seek out fairies, keep company with them and become fairies themselves.

(60) The original Yellow Crane Tower（黄鹤楼）was located on the Yellow Crane Ait（黄鹄矶）at Ezhou（鄂州）Town facing the Great River to the west. It was first built during the Three Kingdoms Period in the second year of Huangwu（黄武二年）of Wu（吴，223）, being burnt down and rebuilt again and again through the centuries. According to one tradition, when Fei Hui（费祎，？– 253）had been metamorphosed into a fairy, he rode off on and alighted from a yellow crane in this tower. Another legend has it that Xun Gui（荀瓌）, once resting in the Tower, saw fairies coming astride cranes

from the southwest, alighting there, holding their feast and flying away afterwards. A third folktale says that the fairy known by the name Wang Zi'an (王子安) had passed the tower several times on the back of a crane.

(61) The cane of green jade was one used by a faery to prop himself or herself.

(62) The Five Mounts of the great Central Empire mean originally Tai, the East Mount (东岳泰山); Hua, the West Mount (西岳华山); Huo, the South Mount (南岳霍山); Heng, the North Mount (北岳恒山) and Songgao, the Central Mount (中岳嵩高). Here, However, they mean in general the noted mountains of the land.

(63) By the side of the South Dipper (南斗星座) or the Little Bear (小熊星座) in contrast with the North Dipper (北斗星座) or the Great Bear (大熊星座).

(64) Folds of mountain ranges are involved like layers of screens wrapping around one another, all enshrouded in gorgeous clouds of brocade.

(65) Poyang Lake (鄱阳湖) which reflects a dark greenish-blue.

(66) The Incense Burner Cliff (香炉峰), and the Double Swords Cliffs (双剑峰).

(67) Golden Portal Peak (金阙岩), also called Rock Gate (石门), is in the southwest of the Incense Burner Cliff.

(68) The Silvery Stream (银河) means the Triple Waterfall (三叠泉) splashing down three-crooked over the Three Rock Beams (三石梁).

(69) The district of Mount Lu during the Spring and Autumn Period (春秋, 722–481 BC) belonged to the kingdom of Wu of the Three Kingdoms.

(70) In ancient geography, as the Great River flowed into Xunyang (浔阳) district, it branched off into nine streams.

(71) Xie Lingyun (谢灵运, 385 – 433), a Six Dynasties poet whom Li Bai esteemed highly, in his poem *Entering the Mouth of Lake Pengli* (《入彭蠡湖口》) has a line "Climbing slopes to watch myself in the stone mirror (攀崖照石镜)." It was said that it could reflect human images.

(72) According to the occult art of metamorphosing oneself into a fairy, a proper quantity of mercury is to be transformed into cinnabar, which is changed back to mercury then the mercury is restored into cinnabar. The process is repeated again and again, until the dosage fourth time restored to cinnabar. Then, swallowing the cinnabar would make one acquire fairyhood.

(73) The Chinese original 琴心三叠 means the complete composure of the mind as being totally free from lay thoughts. When one has reached that absolute quietude, one has obtained fairyhood.

(74) The newly initiated fairy, with a lotus bloom in his arm as a symbol, then goes on his pilgrimage up the Gem Capital Mount (玉京山) to pay homage to the Primeval Heavenly Divinity (元始天尊).

(75) According to *Huainan-zi* （《淮南子》）, a certain Lu Ao （卢敖）, having roamed all over the land, came to Menggu Mountain （蒙谷山）, where he saw a man of novel appearance whirling in the winds. Lu Ao requested him to keep his own company. That man laughed and said, "I expect to meet Han Man （汗漫, a fairy's name） on the outskirts of the Nineth Heaven, and so could not abide with you long." Saying this, he leapt into the coulds. It is known that Lu Ao was a doctor of the First Emperor of Qin （秦始皇时的博士）. Here, Li Bai calls his friend Lu Xuzhou "Lu Ao" and mean himself to be Han Man; he would expect to accompany his friend to rove the empyrean in the not distant future.

This poem was composed by Li Bai in the first year of Shangyuan （上元元年，760） on Mount Lu, the year after he was pardoned by imperial decree from being suspected of implication in the murder of Emperor Su's （肃宗） brother King Yong （永王）. The poet was then sixty years old. He had once taken a landscape-sighting trip to Mount Lu with Lu Xuzhou some years before. After being stricken in that untoward event with imprisonment and exile, he was then in his late years. Besides taking consolation in mountain sceneries, his interest in expecting to metamorphose himself into a fairy had gained on him. Some literary critics tend to say there are traces of his fairyhood in these lines. Two years later, Li Bai died. He had then purged his mortality and become an eternal spirit of poetry ever afterwards.

(76) Another title for this phantasmagoria given by the poet himself is *On Parting with Certain Gentle Friends of East Lu* （《别东鲁诸公》）. The ancient state Lu, the dukedom given by King Wu （武王） of the Zhou Dynasty as a fief to his younger brother Ji Dan （姬旦） in 1046 BC, covering originally 100 square *li*, lay in the southern part of our mordern Shandong Province and the norhtern fringes of today's Jiangsu and Anhui Provinces. This poem was written by Li Bai in the fourth year of the Tianbao （天宝四年，745） period of Emperor Xuan-*zong*'s reign before he left east Lu for his journey to Yue. Although dynasties have passed away, large tract of land has been still known as Lu through the Tang Dynasty even to our modern times.

(77) Mount Tianmu is about 50 *li* (15.1 miles) east of Xinchang *xian* （新昌县）, Zhejiang Province today. According to legendary lore, it was so named on account of the singing of songs by an old heavenly lady heard by someone in remote antiquity. The mountain range regarded by the Taoists as their Sixteenth Region of Bliss （第十六福地）, comes from the Kuocang （括苍） chain spreading over six *xian*. The poet Bai Juyi （白居易） in his *Note on the Wozhou Mount Dhyana Hall* （《沃洲山禅院记》） says, "In the landscape

of the Southeast, Yue (越) is the head, Shan (剡) the face and Tianmu of Wozhou (沃洲, in the east of Xinchang *xian*) the eyebrow and the eye."

(78) In ancient days, Penglai (蓬莱), Fangzhang (方丈) and Yingzhou (瀛洲) were reputed to be the Three Fairy Islands. In the West, fairies are conceived to be diminutive imaginary beings with supernatural powers, able to help or harm human beings. In China, they are supposed to be of ordinary human stature and to have their own supernatural existence and society.

(79) The Five Great Mounts: see Note (62) on "the Great Mount Tai" in Du Fu's *Sighting the Great Mount Dai* (《望岳》).

(80) Crimson Town (赤城) is the southern-most mountain of the Tiantai Range. "Its rocks are red like glowing clouds during sunrise and sunset moments."

(81) Mount Tiantai (天台山): It is in the north of Tiantai *xian* (天台县) in Zhejiang Province. It is the eastern branch of the Xianxia Range (仙霞岭), connected in the southwest with the Kuocang and Yandang (雁荡) chains and in the northwest with the Siming (四明) and Jinhua (金华) mountains. Crimson Town is six *li* north of Tiantai *xian*. Mount Tianmu is in the northwest of Tiantai, overlooking Sheng *xian* (嵊县).

(82) Mirror Lake (镜湖，鉴湖) is in the Shaoxing City (绍兴市), Zhejiang Province.

(83) From this line on, the poem enters the poet's dream world.

(84) Shan Brook (剡溪) is a small stream in the south of Zhejiang's Sheng *xian*; it is the upper stream of Cao'e River (曹娥江).

(85) Sire Xie's (谢公) night hut means the poet Xie Lingyun's (谢灵运，385–433) transcient lodging place where he put up for a night before accending Tianmu Mount the next morning. Xie improved on the ancient clog for wearing on raining days, which had two crosswise teeth or jags, one underneath the upper middle part of the sole and the other near the heel, by eliminating the front jag on the clog for ascending mountain tracks and eliminating the rear jag on the clog for descending mountain tracks. Clogs of such make were called Sire Xie's clogs.

(86) According to *The Tales of Strange Events* (《述异记》), "In the southeast, there is the Peach Capital Mountain (桃都山), on which grows the gigantic tree Peach Capital (桃都) with branches three thousand feet apart. The heaven's chanticleer crows when the sun shines on this tree, and then all cocks on this earth crow in response."

(87) In this line, the poet wakes up from his dream to "probe deep into the realm of Yue."

(88) In remote antiquity of Xia (夏, 2070 – 1600 BC), Shang (商, 1600 – 1046

BC) and Zhou (周, 1046 – 256 BC), Yangzhou (扬州) was one of the Nine States (九州), embracing Jiangsu, Anhui, Jiangxi, Zhejiang and Fujian Provinces at present. As time went on, its domain shrank considerably through the centuries. During the Tang Dynasty, the county Guangling (广陵郡) was also called Yangzhou (扬州). Today, the latter's namesake is in the middle of the province Jiangsu on the northern bank of Yangzi (扬子), the Long River (长江), as a mere city.

(89) The Yellow Crane Tower was a renowned structure in China's literary history. Its site is on the Yellow Crane Ait (黄鹄矶) of the Snake Hill (蛇山) by the northen bank of the city Wuchang (武昌). It was said to be first built in the second year of Huangwu (黄武二年，223) of Wu, one of the Three Kingdoms. Fei Hui (费祎), Wu's general, who lived at the turning of the 2nd to the 3rd centuries, becoming a fairy, was said to often rest the yellow crane he rode on the tower, hence its name. The tower was burnt and rebuilt many times in the nation's chronicle.

(90) The third moon of the lunar calendar is approximately corresponding to April of the Gregorian calendar.

(91) The original 烟花 has never been explained since the poet.

(92) As his dear friend has disappeared his feelings for him flush like the east-flowing torrents of the Long River.

(93) The original of these two and the following two lines 蓬莱文章建安骨，中间小谢又清发 is alluding to the philosophical and literary attainments of the poet's uncle Li Yun and the poetical talent of the poet himself. Li Bai means to say that his uncle Yun, a decreed editor (校书郎) familiar with the philosophical works of Lao-*zi* (老子) and Zhuang-*zi* (庄子), has absorbed the deep, occult wisdom of these two fairy philosophers who have gone to live their eternal lives on the Five Fairy Islands Penglai (蓬莱), Fanghu (方壶), Yingzhou (瀛洲), Yuanqiao (员峤) and Daiyu (岱舆) and is well studied in the literary works of Cao Pi (曹丕), Wang Can (王粲), Chen Lin (陈琳), Xu Gan (徐干), Liu Zhen (刘桢), Ying Chang (应瑒), Ruan Yu (阮瑀) and Cao Zhi (曹植), who lived during the Jianan (建安) years (196 – 219) of Emperor Xian of Han (汉献帝，190 – 220). Speaking of himself, the poet says that his own endowments are comparable to those of Xie Tiao (谢朓，玄晖) of Qi (齐，479 – 502).

(94) In ancient China, a common man, usually a scholar, when given an office of some importance, would as a rule begin to wear an official hat at the ceremony of officiating until the end of his term. When he resigned, it was said that he hung up his hat (of office).

(95) The poet's own note to this poem: "My old friend Jia Chun (贾淳) asks me to question the moon."

(96) The original of this, 丹阙, means "An imposing portal painted with cinnabar", that is a huge, imperial structure of stone blocks so coloured in the form of a gate, by ascending which one, usually an important personage, could command a view infinitely far and wide. The original of these two lines simply gives its reader the powerful but simple impression of the sparkling moon casting its beams upon himself who stands upright on a massive stone gateway of great importance.

(97) Legend has it that there is a white rabbit in the moon which keeps pounding on the elixir of life year in, year out.

(98) The ancient King Yi's (后羿) queen Heng'e (姮娥) has been said to have stolen the elixir of life given by *Xi* Wang-*mu*, the fairy Western Queen Mother (西王母) to the king, and run away to the moon where she lives immortally in eternal loneliness.

(99) The Phoenix Terrace (凤凰台) was in the southwest of the chief town of Jiangning County (江宁府), and is in the southeast of the city Jinling (金陵), now called Nanjing (南京). In the 16th year of the Yuanjia Period (元嘉) of Wen-*di* (文帝) of Song (刘宋, 439) during the Six Dynasties, three multi-coloured birds like peacocks with melodic chantings settled down on the hills, attended by a host of other birds. People called them phoenixes. They sojourned there for some time and flew away. A terrace was built to commemorate the occurrence.

(100) Wu Palaces mean those built by Sun Quan (孙权), the founder of the state Wu, one of the Three Kingdoms, at the beginning of his reign (222 – 252).

(101) The Jin Dynasty was divided into West Jin (西晋, 265 – 317) and East Jin (东晋, 317 – 420).

(102) The Tri-Peaked Mount (三山) is fifty-seven *li* southwest of Jinling City, four *li* around and 290 Chinese feet high. It is actually a small hill, but is exaggerated by the poet to pierce "through the azure sky."

(103) There is a syntactic inversion of the original line 白鹭洲中分二水 into 二水中分白鹭洲 for the sake of rhyme. The Qinhuai River (秦淮河), the confluence of two streams flowing from the two mounts Jurong (句容) and Lishui (溧水), runs in union from Fangshan (方山), through the city Jinling westward into the River, where it dashes on the Egret Ait and is diverged into two currents wrapping round the Ait to run eastward.

(104) The Egret Ait is a little isle on which egrets in great numbers nested at that time.

(105) "The floating clouds" signify libels against the poet to Emperor Xuan-*zong* of Tang.

(106) He is prevented from the sight of the Imperial City; it makes him sad.

(107) The Tower was built by Xie Tiao, High Sheriff of the Country Ning-guo-fu of South Qi (南齐宁国府太守谢朓). Li Bai cherished great admiration for Xie, as evidenced also in his another poem *Humming under the Moon atop the West Tower in Jinling City* (《金陵城西楼月下吟》), although we know he is a much greater poet.

(108) Two currents of water entwine around the town: they are the Wan Stream (宛溪) and the Ju Stream (句溪).

(109) The pair of bridges called the Phoenix (凤凰) and the Jichuan (济川) arch over the Wan Stream. They were built across the water during the Kai-huang years (开皇, 581 – 601) of the Sui Dynasty (隋朝, 581 – 618).

(110) The original 橘柚 (oranges and pomelos) should not be literally translated perhaps, for the latter, we know, would not bear fruit round Xuancheng, Anhui; it could only do so in Fujian, Guangxi, Guangdong, Jiangxi, Zhejiang, Hunan and Sichuan Provinces, where the climate is much warmer. Here two Chinese characters must be employed by the poet: after 橘 there should be another one, to fill in the metre. The choices open to Li Bai were 柑 (*gan*) and 橙 (*cheng*), but he could use neither of them, for they are both of level tones (平声), while here only a character of uneven tone (仄声) should be used, according to the rules of five-charactered *lü* verse (五言律诗) in the "late" prosody of classical Chinese poetry (今体诗) 人烟寒橘柚 (平平平平仄); 秋色老梧桐 (平仄仄平平). So he was forced to pick out 柚 (*you*) (pomelos) to follow 橘 (*ju*) for the sake of tonal euphony.

(111) These two lines convey the sense and tone of the Chinese original 秋色老梧桐, which is a syntactic inversion of 梧桐秋色老 for the sake of rhyme, that is, the platane (leaves) show that the complexion of autumn is old — the fall season is far advanced — with the character 寒 (cold) of the previous original line removed to the end of these two lines in my rendition.

(112) The last two lines of the original as well as of my version consist of a question to be answered. The answer, not given in the poem, is understood: "It is I."

(113) This ancient peopled center high on the mountainside originally called Fish Belly Town (鱼腹城), was in the east of the present Fengjie *xian* (奉节县) of Sichuan Province. Its name was changed into Baidi, meaning the Town

of the White Emperor, by Gongsun Shu (公孙述，? – 36) during early East Han (东汉, 25 – 220) who declared himself the supreme ruler bearing that title for twelve years.

(114)　From Baidi Town to Jiangling Prefecture (江陵府), a *xian* in Hubei Province today, through the 700-*li* Three Gorges (三峡) of the Long River (长江), the waterway bound by interminable cliffs, full of screeching gibbons on both banks, known to be twelve hundred *li* in drift, was said to speed up a light boat in one day.

This masterly stroke of a seven-charactered *jue* quatrain (七绝) was written by Li Bai when he heard unexpectedly the message of his being pardoned by imperial decree at Baidi Town in the spring of the second year of the Qianyuan Period (乾元二年，759) in Su-*zong*'s reign, on his way of exile to Yelang (夜郎) for his enforced involvement in the rebellion of Prince Yong (永王李璘). It breathes of great joy in the high speed of the skiff.

(115)　According to Wang Qi (王琦), the editor of the Qianlong (乾隆) edition of *Li Bai's Complete Works* (1758), the bonze Wang Qian's (王僧虔) *Records of Artistic Skill* (《技录》) mentions *Goodman, Cross Ye Not the River* (《公无渡河》) as one of the thirty-eight tunes or *The Tune of the Zither* (《箜篌引》). *Ancient and Present-day Notes* (《古今注》) has it thus: *The Tune of the Zither* was composed by Li Yu (黎玉), the wife of a Korean quay guard Huoli Zigao (霍里子高). Zigao early one morning propelled his boat for washing himself. A white-haired madcap, holding a water pot and spreading his locks in the winds, attempted to wade the river; his wife ran after to stop him, but too late. The man was immediately drowned; his wife howled out a heart-breaking lament after him, and as soon as it was over, jumped into the river too. Zigao returned home to tell his wife the sight and imitate the tones of the pathetic lament, whereupon, she, deeply moved, composed a tune of lament on the zither after her husband's sad tale and mimicking. It is said that all those who heard the tune could not help being touched to tears. Li Yu taught the tune to a neighbour's girl named Li Rong (丽容), calling it *The Tune of the Zither*.

This poem is regarded by some critics such as Chen Hang (陈沆) and Zhan Ying (詹锳) to be packed with implications from contemporary political events of the poet's time, in which Li Bai himself was involved. When Xuan-*zong*'s imperial prince Li Lin (李璘), Prince Yong (永王), first moved his troops, he was expected by the poet to help put down the rebellion while he appointed himself as his aide-de-camp (府缭佐), but seeing his attempt was but to harass the banks of the River (江) and

Huai (淮), Li Bai ran away to Pengze (彭泽). When Li Lin was put down for his misdeed and dealt with capital punishment, the poet was exiled to Yelang (夜郎) on account of the defamation that he aided Li Lin, but soon pardoned. "The Luteous River … to roar …" is taken to allude to An Lushan's rebellion. Yao in grief heaving his sighs is said to be compared to Xuan-*zong*'s anxiety over the revolt. Su-*zong*'s arduous efforts and his general's aid to suppress the uprising are supposed to be compared to Great Yu's endearvour to overcome the deluge. Li Lin's harassing the banks of the River and Huai is thought to be compared to the old madman's folly in committing suicide and the whole poem is taken to be a metonymical elegy for Prince Li Lin. The web of analogy is spun too thin. So, the poem should rather be read simply as it seems to anyone without all these political implications.

(116) *Er Ya* (《尔雅》), the book of ancient naming and knowledge, consisting of twenty chapters in three volumes, said to be first compiled by Ji Dan (姬旦, ? –1104 BC), the Duke of Zhou (周公) and successively amplified by Confucius (孔丘, 551 – 479 BC), Shusun Tong (叔孙通, 260? – 190? BC) and some disciples of Confucius and Zheng Xuan (郑玄, 127 – 200) of East Han (东汉), and finally annotated by Guo Pu (郭璞, 276 – 324) of Jin (晋) and Xing Bing (邢昺, 932 – 1010) of Song, says the River gushes out from the northwest foot of Mount Kunlun (昆仑), at first in clear streams but becomes brownish yellow in colour midway and along its long course filled with a thousand seven hundred and one streams before flowing out into the sea.

(117) The Gate of Dragon (龙门), also called Yu's Gateway (禹门口), is first mentioned in *Yu's Proclamation of Taxes in Kind* (《禹贡》), a chapter of *Shang Shu* (《尚书》 — *The Book of the Past*), the earliest book of history known to be written by Confucius. It is said in *The Record of Three Qins* (《三秦记》) that thousands of fishes and tortoises gather below the pass between two precipitous mountain crags without being able to dash up the down-pouring torrents; those that could do so would become dragons. The gate is in the northwest of Hejin *xian* (河津县) of Shanxi Province and the northwest of Hancheng *xian* (韩城县) of Shaanxi Province today.

(118) The original of this line when literally rendered is "He bypassed his home, though he heard his child was crying (儿啼不窥家)." It is an age-old saying throughout the centuries that Great Yu conducting the deluge to the eastern sea for thirteen years passed his homestead three times without entering it. The cataclysm in Yao's reign ravaged the valleys of the Luteous River from

2286 – 2278 BC.

(119)　I take the liberty to translate the original 始蚕麻 (to begin to plant hemp and raise silkworm culture) into "to till and sow."

(120)　Liu Bei (刘备), Emperor of Shu-Han (蜀汉) of the Three Kingdoms, once sent his chancellor Zhuge Liang (诸葛亮) the great strategist to Jianye (建业), the capital of Wu, of which the latter said after his observation of its geographical aspects: "The Zhong Heights wind and twist like a dragon and the Rocky Mount squats like a tiger." (锺山龙蟠，石头虎踞。)

(121)　The Six Dynasties founding their capitals in succession in Jianye (建业，建邺) — called Jiankang (建康) in East Jin (东晋) and Jinling (金陵) in Tang, but commonly known as Nanjing today — were Wu, Jin (晋), Song (宋), Qi (齐), Liang (梁) and Chen (陈) from 222 till 589, for 368 years: after the extinction of Wu in 280 till 317, there was a lapse of 37 years, so actually the city was the capitals of the states during the Six Dynasties for 331 years. In the late years of Datong (大同, the middle of the 540's), a boys' ballad prophesied: "(Someone with) Blue silk strings (reins) on a white horse from Shouyang (青丝白马寿阳来)." Not long later, Hou Jing (侯景) broke Danyang (丹阳) and appeared, riding a white horse and curbing it with blue reins.

(122)　The original 白马小儿谁家子 shows the poet's contempt for Hou Jing. Hou was at first a subordinate to General Erzhu Rong (尔朱荣) of North Wei (北魏). Next, he took sides with Gao Huan (高欢) against Erzhu. Then he yielded to Liang in the first of Taiqing (太清) years of Wu-*di* (武帝). Next year, he rebelled and broke down the city Jiankang. In the third year of Taiqing (549), he overcame the inner capital town Taicheng (台城) and Wu-*di* died of hunger and sorrow. He ravaged with burning, massacre and sacked Guangling (广陵), the county of Wu (吴郡), Wuxing (吴兴) and Guiji (会稽) by turns. Finally, he ascended the throne himself, but was defeated by several generals of Liang and killed by his own men.

(123)　The Last Emperor of Chen (陈后主), hearing that the enemy soldiers of Sui (隋) had broken the defense of his capital, struggled with two of his courtiers, who tried to prevent him from getting into the Jingyang Palace (景阳殿) court well, overcame them and got down with two of his favourite imperial concubines Zhang (张贵妃) and Kong (孔贵嫔). However, they were salvaged out of the well by the Sui men as captives. The *Palace Rear Yard Jade-Tree Bloom* (《玉树后庭花》) was one of the songs composed by the Emperor himself and attuned to music.

(124)　At the end of the Qin Dynasty (秦朝), there were Four Hoary Recluses (商

山四皓), all octogenarians, living in seclusion in the Zhongnan Mountain (终南山), also called South Mountain (南山), which are known to have an extent of 800 *li* in length and breadth.

(125)   Zhongnan Mountain (终南山) or the Qin Range (秦岭) is situated in the south of the provincial chief city Xi'an of Shaanxi today, then the capital of the Tang Dynasty. At the time scholars not gone into the official arena mostly lived in their hermitages on this mountain.

(126)   The mountaineer Husi (斛斯山人) was a recluse residing here. He was a descendant subject of North Zhou (北周), one of the three North Dynasties (北朝), a member of the national minority Xianbei (鲜卑).

(127)   This is probably referring to the "Song" attuned to the heptachord strain so named, collected in the *Ancient Garner of Songs* (《古乐府》).

(128)   Hanyang (汉阳) is in the west of Wuchang, on the northern bank of the Han Stream (汉水).

(129)   The Parrot Isle (鹦鹉洲) is in the southwest of the tripartite city Wuhan, in the middle of the Yangzi (扬子) or Long River.

(130)   The Tai Mountain (泰山), also called Mount Dai (岱宗), sprawling across the ancient states Qi (齐) in the north and Lu (鲁) in the south, is in the present Shandong Province. The five Great Mountains of the ancient empire are Tai, the great east mountain (东岳泰山); Hua, the great west mountain (西岳华山); Huo, the great south mountain (南岳霍山); Heng, the great north mountain (北岳恒山); and Song, the great central mountain (中岳嵩山). Of them all, the Tai is the greatest, hence known as the chief of the five mountains, the noble Mount Dai (岱宗).

(131)   The southern sides of the mountain exposed to the sunlight first, are light (阳) first and the northern sides of the mountain shone upon later are shaded (阴) at first.

(132)   This poem was written in about the fifth year of the Tianbao Period (天宝五年, 746) during the Tang Dynasty by the poet when he had arrived not long at the capital Chang'an. It is known in history that Li Bai (李白) with He Zhizhang (贺知章), Li Shizhi (李适之), Li Jin (李琎), Cui Zongzhi (崔宗之), Su Jin (苏晋), Zhang Xu (张旭) and Jiao Sui (焦遂) were all eight of them noted drinkers, known as the "Eight Faeries in Drinking." Although all residing in Chang'an once, they did not do so at the same time. On the fact that they were drinkers alike, Du Fu based his relations. The poem in its verse structure is unusual: every line rhymes and all lines rhyme in concord; there is no beginning, nor end; the lines describing the eight, the numbers of lines devoted to them are not equal,

but at the begining and the end and in the middle, two lines are given to each person, in the fore and hind parts three or four lines are used, with order in variety. Among them all, He Zhizhang was the eldest, being forty-one years older than Li Bai (and fifty-two years' Du Fu's senior), so he is mentioned first of all. The others are named according to their official positions, from princedom through chancellorship to plain commonalty. The sketching of their drunken manners is characteristic individually, with a hidden strain of suppressed feelings.

The translator regrets for not rendering the original into English line by line and failing to use one all-embracing rhyme in all the lines. The Prince of Ruyang and Cui Zongzhi are each given one line: too many than in the original.

(133) He Zhizhang, a native of Yongxing of the state Yue (越州永兴), known as Xiaoshan *xian* (萧山县) of Zhejiang Province today, was the Lord of the Secretariat (秘书监). He was noted for his carefree, unconventional manners, calling himself "the Madcap of Siming" (四明狂客). Having read some of Li Bai's masterly poems, he called his new acquaintance "the Exiled Fairy" (谪仙人); inviting the latter to a tavern, he untied a gold tortoise from his robe band to pay for their drinks for lack of enough ready cash.

(134) The Prince of Ruyang Li Jin (汝阳王李琎) was Xuan-*zong*'s nephew. It was his habitual practice to be thoroughly warmed up with strong drinks before he would attend the morning court of his uncle emperor. He was said to be so fond of alcholic liquors that he would his feudal estate be changed to Wine Spring (酒泉), a county called Jiuquan *xian* (酒泉县) today, in Gansu Province. It was said that under the county bulwark, there was actually a spring having the taste of wine.

(135) Li Shizhi (李适之) became the Left Chancellor (左相) of Xuan-*zong* in the eighth moon of the first year of the Tianbao Period (天宝元年, 742); in the fourth moon of the fifth year (746), he was pressured by Li Linfu (李林甫) off his office and in the seventh moon, demoted to Yichun (宜春) as the High Sheriff (太守) of that county. In the first moon of the next year, he committed suicide by taking poison. This poem of Du Fu was written sometime after Li was removed from his chancellery and long before his poisoning himself. Whales were supposed in ancient days to be capable of sucking and spouting some hundred streams.

(136) Cui Zongzhi (崔宗之), son of the Lord of Imperial Personnel Department (吏部尚书) Cui Riyong (崔日用) and feudal successor to his father as the

Duke of the State Qi (齐国公), was the Lord Attendant of the Imperial (侍御史) and a friend of Li Bai.

(137) Ruan Ji (阮籍，210 – 263), a noted scholar, poet, anchorite and drinker of Wei (魏，220 – 265) during the Three Kindoms, reputed as one of "the Seven Sages of Bamboo Groves" (竹林七贤), was well known for his glinting with the white of his eyes at the vulgar lot to signify his contempt. Here, Cui Zongzhi is allusively sketched as looking down upon the vulgar with sniffing pride.

(138) Su Jin (苏晋), one of the elect in an Imperial Examination during the early years of Xuan-*zong*'s reign, was a devout believer in Buddhism and a vegetarian, but he often became drunk and forgot to observe his dhyana vigils. Buddhist faith prohibits the drinking of wine among its strict believers.

(139) Li Bai was well-known for his prolific outpourings in poety after he had a quart fermented drinks. Once he was intoxicated in a tavern when he was summoned by Xuan-*zong* to appear before his imperial presence in an aloeswood arbour in the palace garden to compose poems for attuning to music. According to Fan Chuanzheng's (范传正) *New Tomb Tablet of Li Bai* (《李白新墓碑》), when Xuan-*zong* was once taking a barge on the White Lotus Pond (白莲池), he summoned Li Bai to write a tale on the occasion when the poet was already drunk at the Imperial Hall of Literati (翰林院); the emperor ordered Gao Lishi (高力士), the General (actually an eunuch), to help bearing the poet to his imperial presence. These incidents and his calling himself "a faery in the realm of spirits" before Xuan-*zong* show how he was in the emperor's high favour and how highly he bore himself.

(140) Zhang Xu, the eminent calligraphic artist, a native of the state Wu, was called the sage of the *cao* mode (草圣) of that art. When he was thoroughly drunken, he would take off his office hat even before princes and lords, howl and dash along, and then wield his brush on silk scrolls, hence known as Zhang the Lunatic (张颠).

(141) Jiao Sui of the commonalty, whose events are not well-known, is said to be reputed for his sparkling eloquence. When he was thoroughly heated up with hard liquors, his companions at the table would be struck with wonder by his brilliant discourse.

(142) This descriptive lyrical ballad was presumably composed by Du Fu in the spring of the 12th year of the Tianbao Period (天宝十二年，753) during the reign of Xuan-*zong* of Tang (唐玄宗). In the 11th moon of the previous year (天宝十一年，752), Yang Guozhong, the so-called brother of the

Imperial Concubine Yang Yuhuan, was decreed the Right Chancellor (右相) by imperial edict. The poem is a hidden satire on the court life with all its exquisite picturesque details. The crux of its sarcasm lies in the three lines (two in the original) "The willow catkins ... to show amour's troth" towards the end. The butt of revulsion is named at the very end to be the big bogy — the new chancellor.

(143) In ancient times, the Celestial Stems (天干：甲、乙、丙、丁、戊、己、庚、辛、壬、癸) and twelve Terrestrial Branches (地支：子、丑、寅、卯、辰、巳、午、未、申、酉、戌、亥) were used as symbols matched in twos and progressing by rotation (甲子、乙丑、丙寅、丁卯、戊辰、己巳、庚午……) to compute the periodic durations of the day, the days, the moons and the years till sixty of the pairs were completed to form a cycle and the process was repeated again and again. It is stated, nowadays, the lunar years are still named in this wise. In the *Ceremonial Records* 《礼仪志》 of *The Late Han Chronicles* (《后汉书》) that on the first *Si* day (巳日) of the year's third moon, officials and the commonalty all go to the eastern stream of Luoyang (洛阳) to purge themselves of dirt and illness. Since Wei (魏，220 – 265) and Jin (晋，265 – 420), the customary practice was fixed definitely on the third moon's third day of the lunar calendar. Among the great many beauties that came to take a spring stroll on the bund of the Zigzag River Pool (曲江池) southeast of Chang'an on the Third Day of the Third Moon, the most prominent were of course the notable sisters of the Imperial Concubine Yang Taizhen (杨太真).

(144) This is an inverted sarcasm.

(145) The original of Du Fu's poem has 蹙金孔雀 here. The four sacred animals of China's traditional lore are *qi-lin* (麒麟，unicorn of monoceros), *feng-huang* (凤凰，phoenix), *shen-long* (神龙，divine dragon) and *ling-gui* (灵龟，prophetic tortoise), peacock being not among them. Although this poem of Du Fu belongs to the "Garner of Tunes" genre (乐府诗) and so need not conform to the prosodic pattern of meticulous distribution of level and uneven tones (平仄声) as it is necessary to do so in a "modern" *Lü* or *jue* poem (今体律绝诗), yet to put the proper 凤凰 here would make the line's tones 仄平仄平平平平 altogether too unbalanced and noisy to its readers' ears; hence he chooses to substitute 孔雀 (仄仄，peacock) instead for the sake of euphony. But in the translation, there is no necessity to render the original literally for no tonal redundancy is involved here, and peacock, in the West, often connotes the idea of vanity, while in China, there is no such allusive meaning. 蹙金 in the original means to embroider

127

with gold thread curled or twisted tight, so as to make the embroidered surface slightly embossed.

(146) There is some difference between China's *qi-lin* and the unicorn or monoceros of the West. *Qi-lin* (specifically, *qi* is the male and *lin* the female) is a mythical animal like the elk in size, but having a single antler and a tail like that of an ox, with its hide covered all over by scales; it is noted for its kindness to other smaller creatures, as very speedy in movement, it would not even step on ants. The unicorn or monoceros of the West is a fabled creature usually represented as a horse with a single spiraled horn projecting from its forehead and often with a goat's beard and a lion's tail; it is often symbolic of chastity or purity. *Feng-huang* in China (specifically, *feng* is the male bird and *huang* the female), also called *yan* (鹧), is the fabulous sovereign of birds. Collected in *Er Ya* (《尔雅》), the earliest lexicon of the world compiled in early Han (汉, 206 BC—AD 220), *yan* or *feng-huang* is explained by its annotator to have the cock's head, the snake's neck, the swallow's chin, the tortoise's back and the fish's tail, with plumes of five hues and over six feet tall. When it appears, there would be universal peace. In the West, the phoenix is a fabulous Egyptian bird of great beauty too, but not so explicitly delineated; it is said to live five hundred years, to burn itself to death and to rise from its ashes in the freshness of youth, and live through another life cycle.

(147) With many-layered sparkling beryl gems strung and dropping down in folds from their raven hair to their temples.

(148) A variant, more common text has 腰极 where, which means 裾 according to *Er Ya*, and this is explained by its annotator Guo Pu (郭璞) as the back overlap of a robe (后裾). In the absence of North Song block print texts, it is more likely that the pearl-studded waist bands make their bodily curves shapely, rather than the back overlap or skirt of their gowns.

(149) According to the *Old Tang Chronicles* (《旧唐书》), the Imperial Concubine had three elder sisters, entitled the State Queens of Han (韩国夫人), of Guo (虢国夫人) and of Qin (秦国夫人), of whom only two are mentioned here in the original for metrical reasons. The State Queen of Han was her eldest sister, that of Guo, her third elder sister (and Yang Guozhong's mistress) and that of Qin, her eighth elder sister, all of whom were entitled in the seventh year of the Tianbao Period (天宝七年, 748). Before the State Queen of Guo was entitled, her husband had already died. The emperor Xuan-*zong* had promiscuous relations with all of them, his most favoured one beside the Imperial Concubine being the State Queen

of Guo, as evidenced by a noted quatrain entitled with her name (《虢国夫人》) written by the poet Zhang Hu (张祜). Priding herself on her natural beauty, she did not resort to cosmetics. Their easy virtue, especially the State Queen of Guo's, casts a satirical light on the chaste, pure qualities of the belles mentioned in line 3, for the three State Queens are the chief ones of the belles, and Du Fu's satire is focused upon them.

(150) While the three Yang sisters, sated with delicacies, are reluctant to raise their chopsticks, their waiting maids keep on busily cutting threads, strips and slices of chickens, ducks, hams and the "choice eight" (八珍) with cutters of tinkling bells (鸾刀).

(151) The horse of Yang Guozhong's seems to be hesitating because before and after him is his retinue of guards and attendants that retard its movement.

(152) These three lines (two in the original) mean obviously that when Yang Guozhong has arrived, carriages and ridden horses are rife, for many are his attendants. The willow fluffs of late spring are spread by the uproarious disturbance to the surface of the Zigzag River Pool (曲江池) and partly settle on the white marsileas. Red handkerchiefs of the ladies' promenading on the bund lost by them are left when dropped on the pathways. These are held between the bills of blue birds flying away. Insinuatingly, these lines mean the secret affair between Yang Guozhong and the State Queen of Guo, which was however known to all in the court, except perhaps the emperor Xuan-*zong* and even among his subjects. But Yang was the chancellor in power; our poet, for safety, could only hint with dubious suggestions. The willow fluffs, falling thick like snow and settling on the white marsileas, are compared to Yang Guozhong who is without a respectable parentage, depending on his disreputable relations with the State Queen of Guo who, in her turn, is the emperor's toy. Yang's birth and personality are such a light stuff as the willow fluffs, for it was known that he was the son of Zhang Yizhi (张易之), the gigolo or kept underling paramour (面首) of the late Empress Wu Zetian (武则天); he as a boy was taken by his mother to the Yang family and was considered a cousin of the Yang sisters. And furthermore, there had been a story of a certain courtier very close to the royal family of North Wei (北魏，386 – 534) during the South and North Dynasties bearing the name Yang Hua (杨华), which means willow fluff, who was forced by the mother queen of the ruler to copulate with her. Fearing that if the secret be known to the king, he would be executed for defaming the ruling house, the man fled to the southern state Liang (梁). The mother queen, pining for her beloved man, framed

129

her *Song of White Willow Fluffs* (《杨白华歌》) to make her palace waiting maids sing in their dances, with snatches like "Willow fluffs are wafted by winds to settle down in a southern home" and "Be it wished that the willow fluffs are picked up by birds' bills to drop into nests," etc.

(153) Meipi (渼陂) was a lake five *li* (about 1.553 miles) in the west of Hu *xian* (鄠县) in Shaanxi Province today, lying southwest of Chang'an, the capital of the Tang Dynasty (唐朝, 618–907). Its water came from Zhongnan Mountain (终南山), with a bank of 14 *li*. At the end of the Yuan Dynasty (元朝, 1206–1368), the lake water was drawn dry by soldiers for catching all the fishes in it, and the dried lake bed had become farms. Now, it has been restored to the original size.

(154) Cen Shen (岑参, *circa* 714 – 770), a contemporary poet of Du Fu and his friend.

(155) This poem is supposed by an annotator to be written by the poet in the 14th year of the Tianbao Period (天宝十四年, 755) of Xuan-*zong*'s reign, when An Lushan, the Hu (胡) satrap, raised his revolt that lasted for seven years, hence 《忧思集》 (*Grieved Am I*) in the original.

(156) This poem was written by the poet in the eighth moon (September) of the 15th year of the Tianbao Period (天宝十五年, 756) or the first year of Zhide (至德元年, 756) not long after his stay at Fuzhou (鄜州), now called Fu *xian* (富县), all alone therefrom to Lingwu (灵武), the court in exile of Su-*zong* of Tang (唐肃宗), who ascended the throne there not long ago. On his way, he was captured by the rebel forces of An Lushan and Shi Siming and taken as a prisoner to Chang'an, the broken capital.

(157) This poem was written by Du Fu in the third moon (approx. April) of the second year of the Zhide Period (至德二年, 757) of Su-*zong*'s reign (756–762), when the poet was a captive of the rebel forces of An Lushan and Shi Siming in Chang'an, the occupied capital.

The third and fourth lines of the original may be interpreted metaphorically; so, lines 5 to 8 of the English version should be rendered thus:

| Aggriéved | bȳ thē tímes' | événts, |

| Thē flów|eȳs tōo shéd | théir teárs. |

| Rēgrét|ing eñfór|cēd pártings, |

| E'eñ birds | chánt sóngs wĩth feárs. |

(158) In the second year of the Zhide Period (至德二年, 757) of Emperor Su-*zong*'s reign, when Du Fu was holding the office "Left Gleaner" (左拾遗), i.e., the vice imperial admonisher of the court, Fang Guan (房琯) was dismissed from his chancellery for the smashing defeat of the imperial

troops under his command by the rebel forces. Our poet, hoping to avert the decree by opining dissent, was actually banished for incurring the wroth of his sovereign from the court to his home at Qiang Village in the south of the Fuzhou (鄜州). These three poems were written during that period.

(159) "Turmoils" (世乱) in the previous line refers to the rebellion of An Lushan and Shi Siming and the political and social chaos resulting therefrom; "disasters", or rather "driftings" (飘荡), to the poet's captivity by the rebel troops and his banishment by Su-*zong* from the court. During this calamitous turbulence of a rebellious war that had already lasted for over a year and while it seemed the Dynasty would be overthrown by the Hu satrap at any moment, our poet, first captured by the rebel forces for less than a year and now that he was not wanted at the court, saw that he could still come back home alive, indeed what a fateful chance it was!

(160) In ancient times, the walls of a village house were quite low. His neighbours, wishing not to come into the house to incommode the family in its pathatic reunion of husband, wife and children, crowded on the walls to show their compassion and heave sighs.

(161) This second one of the three poems expresses the conflicting feelings of the writer: he is compelled by the emperor's order to come home for a visit against his own will during his old age; for this is meted out as a punishment to him for his ill proposed counsel to pardon the chancellor Fang Guan, Du Fu is much concerned with the well-being of the Empire; now that the rebellion is far from being suppressed, his enforced stay at home seems to live by stealth to him.

(162) This is referring to the sixth and seventh moons of the previous year, the first one of the Zhide Period (至德元年, 756), when Du Fu had already moved his family from Chang'an to Fuzhou. In the eighth moon, he went alone for Lingwu (灵武), where he heard the prince royal had ascended the throne as Su-*zong*; he was captured by the rebel troops on the way. In the summer of the next year (至德二年, 757), he freed himself from captivity and went to the court in exile at Fengxiang (凤翔), where he was rewarded with the office of "Left Gleaner". His post as the secondary counsellor was not a big appointment, but he was near his sovereign. His advice to pardon the chancellor, however, soon met Su-*zong*'s ire.

(163) This last poem of the trio relates how the poet's neighbours taking along tankards of wine come to console him.

(164) Driving cocks and hens up to roost on trees was a common practice there and then.

(165)   The village elders all earnestly beg pardon of the poet for their wine's lack of strength; it shows their warm feelings for him. This is due to the millet farms being not amply cultivated on account of the war of rebellion.

(166)   For the supply of enlisted grown-up young men is insufficient, teen-aged boys are often pressed into military service.

(167)   "Shen and Shang" in the orginal refer to two of the 28 constellations in ancient China, which are supposed not to be seen at the same time in the sky. The term is often used as a figure of speech to mean kinfolks or bosom friends yearning in vain for a reunion. Antares and Betelgeuse are assumed here to be the English equivalents.

(168)   The poet's own note on this poem, a literary ballad, says: "Written after the recovery of the two capitals. Though they are recovered, the rebel's forces are still rife."

The rebellion of An Lushan, the Tartar satrap — who was murdered and succeeded by his own son An Qingxu (安庆绪, ? – 759) — and his subordinate general Shi Siming — who broke the siege of Xiangzhou (相州) also called the city Ye (邺城), cordoned off by the Imperial army, and relieved An Qingxu in the second year of the Qianyuan Period (乾元二年, 759) of Su-*zong*'s reign, but before long killed him — was carried on by Shi Chaoyi (史朝义, ? –763), Shi Siming's son, who also murdered his own father in the second year of the Shangyuan Period (上元二年, 761) of Su-*zong*'s reign, but committed suicide after his generals submitted to Tang, thus putting an end to the seven years odd rebellion.

"In the winter of the first year of the Qianyuan Period (乾元元年, 758) of Su-*zong*'s reign, the vast legions of the nine Viceroy Generals (节度使) Guo Ziyi (郭子仪), Li Guangbi (李光弼), Wang Sili (王思理) and others surrounded the city Ye (邺城), occupied by the rebel forces under An Qingxu. In the third moon next year, Shi Siming, who had once yielded to Tang, rebelled again, leading his men from Weizhou (魏州) to succor the city Ye, thus attacking the imperial army on both sides with Shi Chaoyi's men. There was no field marshal to give supreme command to the loyal troops and make concerted action. Six hundred thousand imperial soldiers were put to defeat. Guo Ziyi led his corps to break down the Heyang Bridge (河阳桥) for defending Luoyang (洛阳), the old, eastern capital. But the situation quickly worsened. Luoyang and Tong Pass (潼关) soon became threatened. For averting the critical situation and strengthening the belligerent powers of the state, the Imperial goverment decreed compulsory enlistment everywhere to enlarge the supply of soldiery. All around Xin'an and Shan *xian* (陕县), all inhabitants, regardless of age and sex, were enforced to serve in the troops. The war brought great calamity to the people. Just then, Du Fu was returning to Huazhou (华州) via Luoyang, seeing with his own eyes the people there, after the ravage of the rebel forces during the past two years, were now suffering from the compulsory enlistment and pressed into service by the Imperial army. So he wrote these six pieces: *Xin'an Officer, Shihao Officers, Tong Pass Officer, Parting after Nuptials, Parting during Decling Years* and *Parting sans a Home*, short narrative poems recording the sufferings of the people."

"*Xin'an Officer* gives an account of how the poet, while passing the town, just came upon the *xian* officers pressing enlistments hard. Those of age were already all enforced into military service; so the striplings were driven to the battlefields. The poet highly sympathised with them, but could only, while bearing pain, console and encourage them to augment their morale." — From Xiao Difei's (萧涤非) comments.

(169) Xin'an is Xin'an *xian* (新安县) of Henan Province today.

(170) According to Tang statute from the third year of the Tianbao Period (天宝三年，744), a male person over eighteen years old was regarded a middle youth (中男) and one over twenty-three taken to be an adult (成丁).

(171) As all those having attained adulthood had been draughted, the class of middle youths was now next in order to be pressed into military service for increasing the size of the Imperial army and to cope with the rebellious forces.

(172) The Royal Town means the Eastern Capital of Tang, which had been called the Royal Town during the Zhou Dynasty (周朝，1046–256 BC).

(173) Those boys well taken care of by their mothers were fairly nourished and therefore thickset; they were taken leave off by their dear mothers who cried after they left; other boys who had no mothers, being wretchedly fed, were thus lean and short; they came alone, unaccompanied by mothers, and left alone, without mothers to grieve after their departure.

(174) As the draughted had disappeared eastward along the white water, the leave-taking mothers were still crying, with their groanings echoed by the green hills.

(175) From this line onward to the end, the words were all spoken by "One" of line 2 of this poem, that is, the poet himself. They are words of consolation, explanation and encouragement.

(176) "Heaven and Earth" here alludes obscurely to the Imperial court.

(177) According to *The Mirror for Achieving Civil Equity* (《资治通鉴》) by Sima

Guang and others (司马光等, 1084), Guo Ziyi and eight other Viceroy Generals cordoned off the city Ye, while An Qingxu held it vigilantly to wait for Shi Siming's breaking the siege. As food supplies in the city were exhausted, horses' dung was eaten as food. But the imperial legions were not commanded by a marshal with concerted action. The long siege slackened the morale of the imperial troops. Shi selected his mounted ironsides to rush at the official beleaguerers day and night, sent herculean grapplers to steal the uniforms and insignias of the loyal forces and burned their food and fodder supplies. Thus, the official troops lacked staple and feed. Shi Siming then waved all his men forward for a decisive combat. As all the imperial corps were massed in the north of the river Anyang (安阳河) before they were marshalled in proper order, a terrific cyclone occurred, blasting everything and blackening all heaven and earth. Both armies were frightened, the official forces ran to the south and the rebel to the north. Guo Ziyi led his troops to break up the Heyang Bridge (河阳桥) for safeguarding Luoyang, the eastern capital.

(178)　Bands of our beaten troops come back separately to their camps scattered all about like stars. The trouble is that they are not under a single, unified and concerted command.

(179)　This and the following lines consist of words of consolation and encouragement. At the time, there was a famine among the people, but Guo Ziyi's divisions obtained a huge food supply at the eastern capital.

(180)　This line means that the new recruits are to be trained near Luoyang, the old capital.

(181)　This signifies that their labour would not be heavy: the ditches dug by them would not ooze with water.

(182)　The punitive expeditions against the rebellious forces are righteous.

(183)　In the fifth moon of the second year of the Zhide Period (至德二年, 757) of Su-*zong*'s reign, Guo Ziyi, concurrently a Viceroy General, for his failure to recover Chang'an, the Western Capital (西京), begged his Emperor to depose himself from the Lordship of Construction (司空) to the post of Left of Deputy Chancellorship (左仆射). But by the time when Du Fu wrote this poem, Guo had already been elevated to the post of the Chief Lord of the Secretariat (中书令) or the Right Chancellorship (右相). Yet our poet still calls him here by his previous official post "the deputy chancellor", and says that he would be kind to them the new recruits like a fatherly elder or an elder brother.

(184)　This is the second piece of the poet's descriptive and narrative sketches of the Tang Imperial Army's pressing the populace to enlist for putting down the rebellion of An Lushan and Shi Siming. Du Fu shows his sympathy to the war-stricken public by relating what he saw on his way from Luoyang to Huazhou (华州). The poem is written in five-charactered unrhymed lines.

(185) Shihao hamlet (石壕村) is in the east of Shan *xian* (陕县) of Henan Province.

(186) The city Ye, historically also known as Xiangzhou (相州), is the city Anyang (安阳市) of Henan Province today.

(187) Heyang (河阳), now called Meng *xian* (孟县) in Henan Province, was where the Imperial troops of Tang were massed against rebellious forces of An Lushan and Shi Siming.

(188) The poet's bidding "adieu to the old man alone" shows that the old woman had been pressed into the Imperial army for service.

(189) "Tong Pass was the inevitable narrow throat-like passage of strategic importance leading from Luoyang, the eastern capital, to Chang'an, the western one. In the sixth moon of the 15th year of the Tianbao Period (天宝十五载, 756), when An Lushan's rebel forces attacked the pass, the old general Geshu Han (哥舒翰), commanding 200,000 imperial troops, blocked the Pass to resist. The drawn-out siege lasted for half a year, when Yang Guozhong, the Imperial Concubine's so-called cousin, pressed Geshu persistently to open the rampart and accept the challenge. The outcome was that the imperial army was completely smashed by the Tartar host and overwhelming numbers of the loyal men were drowned in the Luteous River (黄河)." — From notes and comments by Xiao Difei (萧涤非).

(190) The chief officer in charge of keeping watch over the Tong Pass under the generals and superintending construction of the huge bulwark. Tong Pass is in Tong Pass *xian* (潼关县) today.

(191) These two lines are exaggerating statements.

(192) For the second time, for Geshu Han had lost the Pass before.

(193) Obstructive fence of pales of stakes set firmly in the ground for defence.

(194) The western capital means Chang'an.

(195) The original 长戟 was a long-shafted weapon, a little different from a halberd, which in the 15th and 16th centuries in Europe was a combined spear and battle-axe; it was a long spear with a side prong near the top, not a battle axe.

(196) "Taolin (桃林) defeat" means the overwhelming defeat at the combat on the Taolin strategic terrain, west of Lingbao *xian* (灵宝县) of Henan

Province today to the Tong Pass.

(197) This is the first of the three *Partings* written by our poet to record the sufferings of the people during the rebellion of An Lushan and Shi Siming against the Tang Dynasty. Early next morning after the nuptials the previous evening, the bride has to see her groom depart from her as a draftee. The poem is a monologue of the bride to her groom, regretting his enforced departure and yet exhorting him to fulfil his duty, and through her sad, complaining and painful assertions, portrays a good-natured, firm young woman of ill fortune in a feudalistic society.

(198) The stems and branches of raspberry and flax are short and slender; the dodder, clinging to them with tendrils in its growth, cannot thus be long. To marry off one's daughters to such wayfarers as the draftees is to court misfortune.

(199) According to Tang customs, on the third day after nuptials a bride would go with her groom to the cemeteries of his ancestors to do homage to them, then the matrimonial ceremony was considered to be fully accomplished. Now that the newly wed couple had only stayed together for one night, the rites are not yet complete, and so her station is not yet clear.

(200) Father-in-law and mother-in-law.

(201) The original of these two lines means "my parents reared me by hiding me day and night from the sight of strangers," to conform to the rites of feudalistic moral code.

(202) In the male-centered ancient Chinese society, there was a saying that a girl married to a cock would have to follow the cock, and one married to a dog would have to follow the dog. Such is the literal sense of the original line.

(203) This last line expresses her love and devotion for her groom.

(204) This poem gives an account of how an old man with his "offspring all in battles fallen and gone" responds to the drafting and his parting with his dear old mate whom he is not going to see again.

(205) The environs 100 *li* around the imperial city were called the "four suburbs." Here they mean the surrounding region of Luoyang.

(206) Tumen (土门) is in the west of Zhuolu *xian* (涿鹿县) of Hebei Province today.

(207) Apricot Orchard Town (杏园镇) is in Ji *xian* (汲县) of Henan Province today.

(208) The poem is the soliloquy of a homeless soldier scattered "from Xiangzhous's (相州) bad rout," coming back to his native place and levied once more to be the corporal drummer for training the new enlistees.

His deserted homeland is covered with rank wild herbage; his village neighbours are all killed or dispersed elsewhere. After a circuitous walk, he finds out a certain lane, formerly familiar, now quite strange to him. There, the sunshine seems weak and the atomosphere is desolate. Before a shanty, he espies two or three foxes, which, seeing and staring at him, bristle their hair fiercely and screech at him. He encounters one or two aged widows. He takes up his hoe to till a little vegetable plot. And then he thinks of his mother who died of sore need in miserable poverty five years after the first uprising of An Lushan and Shi Siming's revolt in the 14th year of the Tianbao Period (天宝十四年，755) of Xuan-*zong*'s reign.

(209)　This poem was written in the autumn of the second year of the Qianyuan Period (乾元二年，759) of Su-*zong*'s reign, when the rebellion of An Lushan and Shi Siming had already broken out for more than four years. There was actually such a solitary beauty forsaken by her husband when her brothers had been slaughtered with others during the rebellious upheaval and their corpses were not even recovered to be properly buried. And she, though poor, was virtuous and independant, living with her dear maid in a thatched cottage in a vale quite removed from town cooking cypress leaves for food. At the end of the poem, she is pictured as leaning against a tall bamboo in the cold breeze. But meanwhile, the poet has his own state of life and personality in mind in the poem, for some time earlier, he had resigned his official post at Huazhou (华州) and taking along his wife and children, crossed the Long Mounts (陇山) and came to live in poverty at Qinzhou (秦州), at present in Tianshui *xian* (天水县), in the east of Gansu Province bordering Shaanxi Province. There is close similarity between the state and mind of the solitary beauty and his own.

(210)　West of the Hangu Pass (函谷关以西) was called "Within the Pass" (关中). In the sixth moon of the fifteenth year of the Tianbao Period (天宝十五年，756) of Xuan-*zong*'s (唐玄宗) reign, An Lushan's uprising swept the regions of the Tang Empire, West of the Hangu Pass.

(211)　Rose mallow is a tall plant of the Hibiscus (木槿) family bearing rose-coloured pink flowers, which blow at dawn and close at dusk.

(212)　These two lines mean that though she is abandoned by her husband and living in pure poverty, she prefers to remain as she is in her present condition, not considering a second marriage with a well-to-do man of whatever state. This is of course in strict accord with the then current Confucian ethics. Reflecting on himself, Du Fu means to imply that, like this beauty, he would stick fast faithfully to the Tang regime in spite of its precarious pass at present.

(213) These two poems were written by Du Fu in the autumn of the second year of the Qianyuan Period (乾元二年, 759) of Su-*zong*'s reign, when the poet was staying at Qinzhou (秦州) in his travels. Since Li Bai and Du Fu parted from each other in the autumn of the fourth year of the Tian-bao Period (天宝四载, 745) of Xuan-*zong*'s reign at Shimen (石门) of Yanzhou (兖州), now in the Shandong Province, they had not ever seen, though having longed for, each other all along. In the second year of the Zhide Period (至德二载, 757) of Su-*zong*'s reign, Li Bai, having been pressured into service by Prince Li Lin (永王李璘) while he stayed at Mount Lu (庐山) as a recluse, was imprisoned at Xunyang (浔阳), the modern river city Jiujiang (九江) of Jiangxi Province, for his affiliation with the prince's plot of rebellion. In the first year of the Qianyuan Period (乾元元年, 758), he was decreed to be exiled to Ye Lang (夜郎), Tongzi *xian* (桐梓县), of Guizhou Province today. In the second moon of the next year, he was pardoned on his way of exile at the Three Gorges (三峡) of the Yangtze River. Du Fu, staying at Qinzhou (秦州) in his travels, knew nothing of Li Bai's latest happenings. Pining for and sympathetic to his friend, he often dreamed of him and thus wrote these two poems.

(214) In ancient China from time immemorial, emperors, kings, nobilities, officials, scholars and their family members all wore special types of hats peculiar to their social positions. Peasants, labourers, artisans, common servants, theatre actors, and merchants wore no distinct sort of hats. Officials, from the court chancellor and ministers down to the city and town sheriffs, aldermen and village chiefs, all had their particular types of hats in accordance with their respective stations, and they all, down to a certain level, had accoutrements such as the painted or laquered wooden badges signifying official status or titles, and metal (copper, brass or tin) signals mounted on painted poles, borne by their followers who walked by twos before their horse-drawn carriages or page-shouldered palanquins, as their pageants.

(215) In the fourth moon of the third year of the Tianbao Period (天宝三年, 744) in Xuan-*zong*'s reign, Du Fu made the acquaintance of Li Bai at Luoyang, the eastern capital, when the latter had been bestowed on by the Emperor with gold and dismissed as an honoured subject but not given an office. They then visited Liang (梁) and Song (宋) in company, the towns Kaifeng (开封) and Shangqiu (商丘) of Henan Province today. The next year, they traveled together to Qi (齐) and Zhao (赵), the

modern Shandong Province and the region in the southern part of modern Hebei Province, the eastern part of Shanxi Province and the northern part of the Luteous River (黄河) in Henan Province today. They rode and hunted in company, composed poems together and commented on each other's works, loving mutually like brothers. In the autumn of that year, they parted at the county of Lu (鲁郡), now Yanzhou *xian* (兖州县) of Shandong Province, when Du Fu wrote this poem. In it, our poet sighs at their common wanderings in uncertainty and failure to initiate the occult art of fairy *dao* (道), — "being ashamed for their inability to follow Ge Hong (葛洪，283–363)." The last two lines form a counsel to his friend as well as a warning to himself, so, how heart-felt is the friendship between them!

The original 飘蓬 means literally the flying, fluttered raspberry, a weed with leaves like those of willows and little white flowers; in autumn, it withers and is blown about by gusts of wind. It is often compared to those whose residences are uncertain because of unstable occupation. Li Bai and Du Fu, the former senior to the latter by eleven years, were both unlucky in their officiary careers. Taoists thought cinnabar could be forged into elixir for attaining longevity and making one immortal. Ge Hong, theoretician of Taoism, medical authority and alchemist of East Jin (东晋，317–420), called himself Baopu-*zi* (抱朴子) and went up to the Luofu Mountains (罗浮山) for turning cinnabar into elixir. Li Bai aspired fervantly for fairyhood; he had tried his hand at such occult practice; at Qizhou (齐州), he was initiated by ceremony into the inner circle of faithful believers. By the time when this quatrain was written, Du Fu had crossed the Luteous River with Li Bai to go up to Wangwu Mounts (王屋山) to visit the Taoist priest Huagai-*jun* (华盖君), who was however already dead. Highly disappointed, they failed in their attempts to attain fairyhood. Our poet asks his friend, "For whom are you so defiant and arrogant?" (飞扬跋扈为谁雄？) Li Bai was noted for his chivalrous temperament and sword wielding; he had stabbed several men in fits of indignation.

— The above notes are taken from Xiao Difei's *Anotated Selections of Du Fu's Poems* (《杜甫诗选注》)

(216) This poem was written in the autumn of the second year of the Qianyuan Period (乾元二年，759) during Su-*zong*'s reign, when our poet was in his wandering stay at Qinzhou (秦州). Du Fu had four younger brothers, named Ying (颖), Guan (观), Feng (丰), and Zhan (占); at the time the youngest one of them was with him, the other three being at Shandong

and Henan Provinces. Herein are expressed his longings for his three other brothers and his native soil, pining at their being drifted elsewhere and his and their common home having vanished on account of the war of rebellion. Under the current martial law, when the night watch drums were struck, no pedestrians were allowed to walk on the streets. Wild geese usually fly in ranged files. To say one solitary brant is screaming in its flight over the border is symbolizing his own state of mind, which is missing the company of his three younger brothers. The night when this poem was written, it happened that the autumnal White Dew Period (白露节，one of the 24 climatic periods of the lunar year) commenced that night, which was September 8 on the Gregorian calendar. The turning of the season all the more deepens the feelings of our poet. The moon shines everywhere with the same lustre. To say that it glows particularly bright at home is of course due to his yearnings for home. With his brothers scattered elsewhere, if he still has a home at his native land, he could yet know their well-beings or ill hap by writing to their common old home; but now that there is no more that old home, he has nowhere to inquire of whether they are still living or dead. And it is further to be grieved that the campaign to suppress the rebellion must be carried on indefinitely long.

(217) This poem was written by Du Fu in the summer of the first year of the Shangyuan Period (上元元年，760) of Su-*zong*'s reign after four years' driftings from Tongzhou (同州) via Mianzhou (绵州) to the western suburb of Chengdu (成都), where, as it was not yet ravaged by the war of rebellion, by the side of the Brocade-Washing River and Flowery Runnel (浣花溪，濯锦江，百花潭), our poet, with the aid of his good friend Yan Wu (严武，726–765), put up his thatched cot and began to lead a long-wished-for life of peace. The poem, showing the tranquillity of the writer's mind, is uncommon in his works. But in the last two lines our readers are reminded by the poet that he is not completely carefree: He has to depend on the kindness of a friend in helping him with a small portion of his office rice.

(218) This poem was written by Du Fu in the summer of the first year of the Shangyuan Period (上元元年，760) during Su-*zong*'s (肃宗) reign of the Tang Dynasty. It first describes closely the exquisite state of his thatched cot, and then, turning the tip of the brush, proceeds to his destitute living, and at last, holding fast to his integrity, declares that he has not waived his fortitude to flatter power or debase himself.

(219) Ten-thousand-*li* Bridge (万里桥), a little stone one, is outside the South

Gate（南门）of Chengdu（成都）, where, during the Three Kingdoms Period, Zhuge Liang（诸葛亮，181–234）, the great statesman, strategist and chancellor of Shu-Han（蜀汉）, saw Fei Hui（费祎，？ – 253）off as imperial emissary to Wu. Du Fu's thatched cot was in the west of the Bridge.

(220) The original 百花潭 (Hundred Flowers Deep Pond) is purposely translated into its present form to avoid mentioning two names both with numbers, which in the Chinese original appear not monotonous but a desired verbal parallel. The Multiflorous Deep Pond was in the south of the thatched cot, which was situated in the north of it. Flower-Washing Pool（浣花溪）, also called the Brocade-Washing River（濯锦江）; Du Fu's thatched cot was situated in the north of it.

(221) Canglang Stream（沧浪江）is a tributary of the Han River（汉水）, celebrated for its limpidity in ancient history. It was mentioned earliest in the chapter *Yu Gong*（《禹贡》）of *Shang Shu*（《尚书》, *The Book of the Past*）, written by Confucius（孔子，551–479 BC）himself. In *The Analects of Mencius*（《孟子》）, it is recorded that a boy sang a snatch of folk song about it thus:

> 沧浪之水清兮，
> 可以濯我缨；
> 沧浪之水浊兮，
> 可以濯我足。

> When the water of Canglang is limpid,
> I could wash with it my hat's chin strips;
> When the water of Canglang is turbid,
> I could wash with it my twain soiled feet.

(222) This alludes to his old friend Yan Wu（严武，726–765）, Duke of the State Zheng（郑国公）. When our poet first came to Chengdu, Yan helped him amply with his sovereign grants of office remuneration. But as these friendly gifts petered out, he, without his own resources, and his family had to suffer from starvation. His ill-fed children appear sallow and dismal in complexion.

(223) And yet he was not at all cowered by poverty, but was as ready as ever to express his uncommon, independent views on matters of the state and the society, though that might get him into trouble and hasten his death.

(224) He is prouder of and laughs at himself, the older he becomes, regardless of what the world thinks of him.

(225) The poet's own note on this seven-charactered *lü*（律诗）octave is "Pleased

to have His Honour the town sheriff Mr. Cui's (崔明府) call on me." The tone of this poem is full of heartiness and candour.

(226) This poem was written in 761 as a cry of the poet in his wretched circumstances for the urgent but vain wish that poor scholars like himself be supplied with ample provisions of food and lodging, so as to enable them to carry on their intellectual pursuits for the benefit of society.

(227) In 756, Dang-xiang-qiang (党项羌) and Tu-yu-hun (吐谷浑) (chieftains of these tribes in ancient China) made constant intrusions into the territory of the Tang Dynasty. The Tang army, being unable to put up an effective resistance, could only ride roughshod over the common people. Their atrocities are strongly condemned by the poet.

(228) These two quatrains, rendered here into English as two octaves, were written by Du Fu in late spring when he had returned to his thatched cot in Chengdu. After his tortuous and aimless wandering for three years, when he had seen Yan Wu, Governor and Duke during Su-*zong*'s reign and Du Fu's friend and superior, off to the court, our poet was struggling along in poverty at Zizhou (梓州) and Langzhou (阆州). Now that he is in more comfortable circumstances, he feels all the more poignantly the beauty of his natural surroundings. Yet, facing all such scenic delights, he cannot but be stirred up with nostalgic thoughts.

(229) Du Fu wrote this poem in Zhongzhou (忠州) in the year Yongtai (永泰, 765) of Dai-*zong*'s (代宗) reign. Yu's temple was in the south of Linjiang *xian* (临江县), two *li* from the river Min (岷江).

Great Yu of Xia (夏禹), the first king of the dynasty, was the grandson of Zhuanxu (颛顼), who was said to have ruled for 78 years and was himself the grandson of the Luteous Emperor (黄帝轩辕氏), the earliest legendary *Di* of the Han (汉) majority of the Chinese race. Yu was ordained by *Di* Shun (舜帝) to be his imperial successor for his splendid achievements in conducting the deluge of the flooding Luteous River (黄河) that ravaged its banks for eight years from 2286 to 2278 BC to the eastern sea. It was common knowledge among China's school boys and girls before the middle of this century that Great Yu passed thrice the entrance of his homestead in eight years without entering it, while he was engaged in the expulsion of the flood. This great benefactor of the Han majority of the Chinese race ruled only eight years on his throne. He died in his inspection tour in 2197 BC at Guiji (会稽). The lunar Xia calendar inaugurated by Yu on his ascension to his throne is still partially in use in China today.

(230) According to the chapter *Yi and Ji* (《益稷》) of *Shang Shu* (《尚书》, *The*

Book of the Past), Yu said "I ride the four vehicles." These are explained in Sima Qian's *Chronicles* (《史记》) as cart for conveyance on land, boat on water, sleigh (橇) on muddy terrain and palanquin (樏楄) for ascending elevations.

(231) According to the primal studies in the earliest anthology of ancient Chinese poetry entitled *Poetry* (《诗》), now known as *The Classic of Poetry* (《诗经》), the 305 poems collected in that anthology early in the Zhou Dynasty (周朝，1046–256 BC) are capable of being specified into six categories according to their nature, namely: popular ballads or folk songs garnered in its early halcyon days (风), lyric poems composed by its intellectuals (雅), odes on happenings of state magnitude (颂), expansions on themes of memorable affairs or occasions (赋), similitudes or comparisons between notable happenings of the past and the present (比), and musings or contemplations on the past, present and future of oneself and the state (兴). *Eight Octaves on Autumnal Musings* (or Meditations) are a series of seven-charactered *lü* poems (律诗) composed by Du Fu at Kuizhou (夔州) in the first year of the Dali Period (大历元年，766) of Dai-*zong*'s (代宗) reign during the Tang Dynasty. They are the product of broodings on autumn, hence Autumnal Musings. From the second year of the Qianyuan Period (乾元二年，759) of Su-*zong*'s reign, when Du Fu left officialdom to reside at Qinzhou (秦州) till now, he had spent in all seven years, leading a wandering life. During these years, the war to suppress the rebellion went on ceaselessly. Now, as the clime was desolate, our poet could not but be sorely moved by his deep concern for the current rule as a loyal subject, from which his personal dejection and self commiseration also arose. The lines "I use to yearn for the capital neath the Great Bear" in the second octave and "I think of my native soil as an absentee" in the fourth are the key statements of all these verses.

The structure of these *Eight Octaves* could be divided into two portions, with the fourth one as the transitional stanza. The first three dwell on Kuizhou first and then think of Chang'an, the capital, while the last five think of Chang'an first and then reflect on Kuizhou; in the first three, the musings shift from reality to reminiscence, and in the last five, the musings flit from reminiscence to reality. And between the stanzas, the starts and ends are well connected, not interchangeable, the eight forming a concerted whole. *Eight Octaves on Autumnal Musings* thus form a featly executed masterpiece of Du Fu, either imbuing sentiments in scenic aspects, or motioning past events to signify the present, or stating current happenings without disguise, or stopping short just on the point of speaking, — the readers must peruse carefully to catch the illusive poetic essence.

(232) The first octave writes about the autumnal scene and the poet's feelings of wanderings and nostalgic thoughts for his native soil. The atmosphere of the Wu Mounts and Gorges around the Great River is desolate and depressive. Du Fu was at Yun'an (云安) last autumn and is here at Kuizhou this one; so, from the time he left Chengdu, chrysanthemums have flowered twice, with his tears also shed twice. He commits his hopes of returning to the capital to a single boat. Thinking of the pressing need of winter garments for the oncoming cold season everywhere and of the thick laundry clubbings before dusk in the high mountain town Baidi (白帝), meaning "the White Emperor," the poet is all the more overcome by nostalgia.

The ancient peopled center high on the mountainside originally called Fish Belly Town (鱼腹城) was in the east of the present Fengjie *xian* (奉节县) of Sichuan Province. Its name was changed into Baidi, meaning the Town of the White Emperor, by Gongsun Shu (公孙述, ?BC–AD 36) during early East Han (东汉, 25–220) who declared himself the supreme ruler bearing that title for twelve years.

— The above and following notes and comments are culled and translated from Prof. Xiao Difei's (萧涤非教授) thorough studies.

(233) In this second octave, the poet writes on the desolate sight of dusk at Kuizhou and his yearning for the capital Chang'an. Every night, he relies on gazing at the Big Dipper to yearn for the imperial city, which he could not see, but was, as it is, now called Xi'an, just under the Big Dipper. Ursa Major, a constellation in the region of the north celestial pole, near Draco and Leo, containing the seven stars that form the Big Dipper, is called the Big Bear in the West. According to *Notes on The Water Classic* (《水经注》) by Li Daoyuan (郦道元, 466 or 472?–527) of North Wei (北魏, 386–534), a fisherman's song had

Amongst the gorges three of Ba-*dong*,
　　The Gorge of the Wu Mounts is long;
At the sad wailings of gibbons thrice,
　　One's tears drip down to wet his gown.

("巴东三峡巫峡长，猿鸣三声泪沾裳"). It is said in Zhang Hua's (张华, 232–300) *The Record of Strange Strands, Rare Things and Unusual Events* (《博物志》) that old traditions have it that the Heaven's River (天河, or Silvery Stream, 银河, i. e., the Milky Way) could be reached by the sea, that of late years there have been people who lived on islets in the sea, every year in the eighth moon there were floating rafts coming in time regularly, people getting on the rafts with food supplies went away for some ten odd days and reached the Heaven's River. Also, according to *The Daily Records of Things and Events in Jing and Chu* (《荆楚岁时纪》) by Zong Lin (宗懔) of Liang (梁, 502–557), Emperor Wu-*di* of Han (汉武帝, 140–88 BC) ordered Zhang Qian (张骞, ? –114 BC), the great general, to trace the Luteous River (黄河) to its source; taking to the raft, he reached the Heaven's River at last after a number of months. Line 4 above is making use of these two allusions to indicate the poet's relations with the court, likening Zhang Qian to Yan Wu and Zhang's reaching the Heaven's River to Yan's returning to the court. Before Du Fu wrote the *Eight Octaves*, he, as a counselor (参谋) to Yan Wu, was a member of the Imperial Secretariat (尚书省，检校工部员外郎). He had formerly entertained the hope of returning to the court in the retinue of Yan Wu. But Yan's death had dashed his expectation of going back to Chang'an — "toward heaven to repair."

In the Secretariat Ministry (书省＝尚书省), according to *The Official System of Han* (《汉官仪》, Han (206 BC–AD 220), written by Ying Shao (应劭, *circa* 153–196) of Late Han (后汉, 25–220), now nonexistent), the walls of the main official halls were plastered with white lead powder and painted with figures of ancient sages and heroic women. When the imperial secretaries attended their offices, they were waited upon each by two attendant ladies holding an incense burner. During Tang, the practice still held as in Han. Du Fu had in the past served in the office of Left Gleaner (左拾遗), which belonged to the Ministry of Attendance and Counsellorship (门下省). He was demoted for his untimely counsel to Emperor Su-*zong* to pardon Fang Guan (房琯) the chancellor for the smashing defeat of the imperial troops under his command by the rebel forces at the Battle of Chentao Marsh (陈陶泽), with 40,000 men completely wiped out. As a subordinate to Yan Wu, Duke of the State Zheng (郑国公), Du Fu was recommended to the office of Overseeing and Examining in the Department of Imperial Works (检校工部员外郎), which belonged to the Secretariat Ministry. Yan's death and the poet's own illness prevented him from attending the secretariat at Chang'an.

And at the limed parapet of Baidi's mountain town tower, he listens to the sad Tartar pipe vaguely moaning in the distance, which means the war of quelling the rebellion is still going on. The last two lines show that after the sun turning west in the first line, the poet has stood ruminating so long that the moon has already cast its sheen on the wisteria over the stones and the white rush flowers of the isle.

(234) In the third octave, the poet writes of the morning scene of Kuizhou and sighs on his good parts unappreciated and of no avail. The mountain town is that of Baidi (白帝城). All around the storeyed riverside house, there were the undulating verdant mountaintops and vales — the expanse of rolling green. Nightly, the fishing boats float along carefree, in contrast to his enforced stay. The early autumn swallows, soon to migrate southward, seem to insinuate to him by their flitting about, that he could not go south to Chang'an, the capital. Kuang Heng (匡衡), a noted scholar of Confucian classics in West Han (206 BC–AD 25), was a chancellor of Yuan-*di* (元帝, 48–33 BC) and was ordained Marquis of Le'an (乐安侯). Often dissenting from his emperor's views on matters of state, he used to quote the classics in support of his own opinions. While his prototype Kuang Heng got encouragement from his sovereign Yuan-*di* of West Han for his dissenting counsels, Du Fu's own efforts to ask pardon from Su-*zong* for the chancellor Fang Guan's (房琯) smashing defeat by the rebel forces of An Lushan and Shi Siming — sustaining a total loss of 40,000 men at the Chentao Battle — resulted in the loss of his own post as the Left Gleaner. Liu Xiang (刘向, 77–6 BC) was also an eminent scholar of Confucian classics and a literati as well as a notable bibliographer of West Han. His son Liu Xin (刘歆, ? –23) continued his heritage as an eminent scholar of the classics, a distinguished bibliographer and an astronomist to boot. Du Fu's grandfather Du Shenyan (杜审言, ? – after 705) was a noted poet before him, but certainly not such a great one as he was. Here, our poet is polite in underestimating himself, speaking of the failure of his own aim. In these two lines, our poet tells his readers what he is thinking of in his solitude besides the longings for his sovereign and the court. And finally, he goes on to reflect on his erstwhile fellow students, who have all become darlings of Fortune now. In the original, the Five *Ling* (五陵) of the Han Dynasty (汉, 206 BC–AD 220) — Chang *Ling* (长陵), An *Ling* (安陵), Yang *Ling* (阳陵), Mao *Ling* (茂陵) and Ping *Ling* (平陵), the five settlements of rich families removed from all over the country to the capital to reside in — are spoken of to signify with irony the well-favoured families of the present with their light, fur-lined robes and fat horses (轻裘肥马).

(235) This fourth octave is the turning point — while the previous three dwell on Kuizhou, this and the following four expatiate on Chang'an. The capital, after its capture by the rebels, its tribulations and recovery, bears no more

the complexion of its past. Du Fu speaks of "these hundred years" in the original second line as a gross number to exaggerate their length, whereas actually the revolt of An Lushan and Shi Siming broke out in 755, only eleven years before the first year of the Dali Period (大历元年, 766) when these octaves were written. My rendition is nearer the reality. The homes of nobilities, after the capital's fall and the tribulations, have all changed their masters; also, after the rebellion, the newly entitled and fresh crop of notables are engaged in setting up their new mansions, vying with one another in luxury and magnitude. At that time, Su-*zong* (肃宗) and Dai-*zong* (代宗) both entrusted their state affairs in eunuchs, giving them great power in military and political matters. Courtiers were divided into cabals and cliques, vying with one another and intriguing with the eunuchs. There was also a group of illiterate enlisted chiefs, waiting at the "Hall of the Viruous" (集贤院) and known as scholarly courtiers. Such phenomena were unknown in the past, hence "none of years ago." The beating of drums (击鼓) and the clanging of gongs (鸣金) were orders of onward attacking and backward retreating in the army, meaning that warfare was rife. "The messages of westward campaigns," with birds' tail plumes stuck in them, means the report is urgent for suppressing the rebellious forces and repelling the penetration of Tubo (吐蕃) hordes. The first six lines speak of Chang'an and affairs of the state, while in the seventh line our poet comes back to himself in Kuizhou. Like fish and dragons, he is submerged here as if in the autumnal river water cold; and here, he is full of feelings and reflections of his vicissitudes.

(236) This octave dwells on the magnificence of the capital's sights and atmosphere, and the notable state of the court. It is thus what is thought of in the first place by the poet among other things as a zealous courtier. The Penglai Palace, meaning that of the fairies, was on the Dragon Head Plain (龙首原) in the northeast of Chang'an, facing southward the Utmost South Mountains (终南山). The Golden Pillar was a stem 200 feet high supporting a big basin of seven embraces in circumference, the whole thing made of brass, with a "fairy's palm" in the basin for collecting dewdrops, which, when taken with gem particles, were supposed to give infinite longevity to a person. The structure was ordered to be fabricated by the Han emperor Wu-*di* (汉武帝, 140–86 BC), a stalwart believer in fairyhood, and erected in the west of the Jianzhang Palace (建章宫) of Han's imperial group of structures. During the Tang Dynasty, though the capital was still Chang'an as in West Han, there was no more the dew-

collecting basin and its stem. Du Fu simply makes use of its fictitious or merely historical existence to give a halo of magnificence to the Tang capital. Dame Wang of the West (西王母) was a fairy lady inhabiting by the Gem Pool (瑶池) on the Kunlun Mountains (昆仑山). According to *The Chronological Book of Bamboo Strips* (《竹书纪年》), King Mu (穆王, 1001–946 BC) of the Zhou Dynasty (周朝, 1046–256 BC) rode up the Kunlun Mountains in the 17th year (1017 BC) of his reign to visit the fairy Dame Wang and was cordially entertained by her. Here and in the next line, our poet imagines a legendary saying and a traditional lore to be connected with Chang'an to give it importance.

Lao-*zi* (老子, 604? – 531 BC) — reputed the earliest great thinker of the Chinese race, the senior sage of the Spring and Autumn Period (春秋, 770 – 476 BC), elder contemporary of Confucius (孔子, 551 – 479 BC) and official compiler of the chronicles in the regal library of the Zhou Dynasty (周朝守藏室之史), of whom Confucius once asked instruction of ceremonials, — whose name is known to be Li Er (李耳) and whose tract Lao-*zi* (《老子》) or *The Dao-de Classic* (《道德经》) consists of 5,000 odd characters on the conformity of human thinking and acts to the law of Nature, is here extolled by Du Fu in alluding to his going from Luoyang in the east westwards through Hangu Pass (函谷关), riding a cart drawn by a bluish dark ox, when the Pass-keeping governor Yin Xi (关令尹喜) observed in advance a purple aura moving westward from the east, signifying the approach of a sage, and on his arrival at the Pass, being requested by the high official to set down his metaphysical deliberations in the occult tract now known to us as *The Dao-de Classic*.

The large fans mounted on poles and made of pheasant tail plumes were ceremonial means or appendants in the court hall, employed to cover up the emperor's sight from the looks of the attending courtiers before he sat down. When he had sat down above facing the kneeling courtiers or retired from their sight under the cover of the fans, these were taken away and put aside. During the Tang Dynasty, the ceremonial court rite for the emperor to sit at the imperil assemblage was early before daybreak; so the first beams of dawn on the figure of the monarch would show his complexion. And then, the reader is told of how the poet finds himself, being fatefully struck down, lying beside the Great River, coming to, all of a sudden, so late in the autumn (as well as during his declining years, for he is fifty-five years old now). In the last line, he wonders how many times (seldom rather than often) he was summoned at the roll call by the portal (青琐, which was incised with designs of interlinked rings that were filled with bluish green pigment) of the yard of court hall to appear before the imperial majesty of Su-*zong* as his Left Gleaner.

(237) In this octave, our poet recalls the past festive splendour of Xuan-*zong*'s imperial visits to the Zigzag River Pool (曲江池) in the southeast of Chang'an, the capital. It is what is thought of by Du Fu in the second place, as he pines on the chaos caused by the rebellious uprising of An Lushan and Shi Siming. Du Fu, now staying at Kuizhou which is in the west of the Qutang Gorge, the first one of the Three Gorges of the Long River (长江), is harking back at the good old days when he was at Chang'an. The site of the Zigzag River (this being its first, original name) Pool bank, today in the southeast of Xi'an, the chief city of Shaanxi Province, was named Spring-Befitting Grove (宜春苑) during Qin (秦，221 – 206 BC), called Pleasure-Roaming Plain (乐游原) in Han (汉，206 BC – AD 220), changed into Hibiscus Garden (芙蓉园) in Sui (隋，581 – 618) and excavated during the Kaiyuan years (开元，713 – 741) of Tang and renamed the Zigzag River Pool. As a spring pleasure resort, it was in the south of Chang'an and east of the Vermillion Bird Bridge (朱雀桥) and in the vicinity of the Pleasure-Roaming Garden, Apricot Garden (杏园) and Maternal Love Monastery (慈恩寺). During the An-Shi (安史) revolt when Chang'an was occupied by the Tartar satrap and his deputy's troops, the scenic spot was in the main ruined. More than sixty years after the An-Shi rebellion was suppressed, efforts were made to rejuvenate the architectural beauty of the scene in Wen-*zong*'s reign (826–841), but the destruction was too overwhelming and attempts at restoration proved to be of no avail. And then, toward the end of the Tang Dynasty, after the capital was taken place of by Luoyang, the River water stopped to flow thither, so the Qutang Gorge mouth and Zigzag River bank, far away from each other, are exaggerated here to be ten thousand *li* apart in the original. In this autumnal season, war fires have linked them together. Xuan-*zong* had orderd to be built the "Tower That Has Flowers-and-Sepals Mutually Shining on Each Other." In the 20th year of the Kaiyuan Period (开元二十年，732), a high-walled passage was built leading from the "Flowers-and-Sepals-Shining-upon-Each-Other Tower" (花萼相辉楼) to the Zigzag River Pool bank for His Majesty to pass through unobserved by his subjects. To Hibiscus Garden, went the sad news of border war combustibles of An Lushan's rebellion. The Zigzag River Pool bank in this octave is full of palaces and towers; in line 5, a swan alighting there would

find itself lost among those structures, and in line 6, flying gulls would be frightened by such a host of masts and riggings on the Zigzag River Pool. These four lines, from the third to the sixth, describe the flourishing state of the Zigzag River Pool and its bank in the past. But alas! The thriving atmosphere and glamorous sights of the bygone days are no more to be found. And in the last line, the reigning sovereign and his successors are reminded with warning that this old terrain "within the Pass" has been from ages past the domain of our memorable emperors and kings, "those of you who follow in their steps should remember their illustrious deeds and examples; you should not divert from their straight, upright paths to indulge in dissolution, ill deeds and wanton policies, in order to avoid this goodly domain fallen into battlefield ruins."

(238)　Kunming Lake, twenty *li* (6.214 miles) southwest of Chang'an and forty *li* (12.428 miles) in circumference, was dug in the third year of the Yuan-shou Period (元狩三年，120 BC) of Wu-*di*'s (武帝，140–86 BC) reign of Han by imperial decree for drilling fleet fighting. No more existent today, it was there in the southwestern suburb of Tang's capital as our poet remembers it here. In the Pool, two stone effigies were erected, the Cowherd (牵牛) in the east and the Shuttle Girl (织女) in the west to represent the stars Altair and Vega, south and north of the Silvery Stream (银河), the Milky Way. In Chinese mythology, the couple meet each other only once in the seventh night of the seventh moon every lunar year when the Maid crosses the bridge formed by magpies linking one another by beaks and tail plumes to meet her lover. The stone figures still existent, are buried underground. The Shuttle Girl does not weave in moonlit nights perhaps because then the star could not be seen with naked eyes. The jade whale was said to be agitating its tail and fins during thunderstorm; it is now preserved in the Provincial Museum in Xi'an (西安). In lines 5 and 6, the poet's thoughts wind on what he sees in imagination in the plants, zizania and lotus cupules, on the Kunming Lake. In the last two lines, he comes back to the inaccessible distance between the court of his sovereign and himself, and finally, to his lone and forlorn state as a solitary fisherman.

(239)　In this, the last one of the *Eight Octaves*, Du Fu dwells on his enjoyment of the scenic beauty of Meipi (渼陂), which consists of the fourth topic of what he thinks of in these strains. In the previous three stanzas, he recalls the Penglai Palaces, Zigzag River Pool and Kunming Lake, all of which are affairs of the court. But in this last stanza, he is reminiscent of his personal enjoyment of the relevant scenic beauty. Kunwu (昆吾) and Yusu (御宿)

were two spots in the southeast of Chang'an, anciently in the extensive Imperial Park (上林苑) of the Han Dynasty. To go from Chang'an by the circuitous way through Kunwu and Yusu to Meipi, one reached finally Meipi the Lake scene, the source of which was the Zhongnan (Ultimate South) Mountains (终南山), today in the west of Hu *xian* (户县) of Shaanxi Province. When Du Fu was in Chang'an, he in the company of Cen Shen (岑参), Gao Shi (高适), Chu Guangxi (储光羲) and Xue Ju (薛据), took a trip to Meipi and all composed poems on the occasion. Du Fu wrote his *The Lay of Meipi* (《渼陂行》). Purple Pavilion Peak (紫阁峰) is a peak of the Zhongnan Mountains, deriving its name from the fact that early in the morning, the glow of sunrise shining on it casts a purple halo thereto to make it look like a pavilion. In the original 香稻啄馀鹦鹉粒，碧梧栖老凤凰枝，there are syntactical inversions for the sake of tonal reasons in the make-up of characters. These two lines describe the beauty of the products of Kunwu and Yusu. "Fairy companions" (仙侣) are meant for the companies enjoying their spring trips to Meipi, the beauty of which is like that of the fairyland, hence the expression. Du Fu here refers to his submitting two pieces of *fu* (赋) to Xuan-*zong*, the Emperor, in the ninth and tenth years of the Tianbao Period (天宝九载，十载，750–751) of his reign, attracting the previous emperor's attention. He was deprived of the office of Left Gleaner by the present emperor Su-*zong*, for his attempt to ask pardon for the chancellor Fang Guan (房琯), who had suffered a smashing defeat and lost 40,000 men under his command, slaughtered in the Battle of Chentao with the rebellious forces of An Lushan and Shi Siming. The last two lines turn back to himself as a summary: the upper one recalls his favourable notice by Xuan-*zong* for his literary merits, while the lower one says that though poverty-stricken, trod by luck, habituating himself to a lone, strange town in his old age, he is still fervently cherishing his dear native soil and harking back for the welfare of the state.

(240) This poem was written by Du Fu in the winter of the first year of the Da-li period in Dai-*zong*'s reign (代宗大历元年，766) when he was staying in the night at the West Pavilion (西阁) of Kuizhou (夔州). Spending his wandering days in this desolate, remote mountain town, the poet, overlooking the magnificent night scene in the Gorges and hearing the sad, heroic horns and drums, became filled with overpowering feelings. The poem is deeply plaintive in tone. Writing here far away from home, he calls it "the horizon." The screeching horns and pulsating battle drums tore the broad silence of night air. The Milky Way is commonly known in

China as the Starry or Heavenly Stream. Thousands of families mourning and wailing in the wild for the loss of their sons refer here to the war of rebellion; the woodcutters and fishermen of the minority groups singing their folk songs are thought of, together with the mourning families, by our poet in his rumination of sleepless night. "The Lying Dragon" (卧龙) means Zhuge Liang (诸葛亮，181–234), great statesman, strategist and premier of Shu-Han (蜀汉) of the Three Kingdoms. The "Galloping Horse" (跃马) refers to Gongsun Shu (公孙述，? –36), a prefecture governor general (太守) of Shu (蜀郡) during the Pretender Wang Mang's (王莽) usurpation (9–23), who declared himself emperor at the end of Wang's reign and was crushed by Emperor Guangwu (光武帝，25–58) of East Han's (东汉) forces in the 15th year of his reign and killed. Both Zhuge Liang and Gongsun Shu had wielded activities at Kuizhou in their own times and both had left their memorial sites there. So, Du Fu, thinking of them, comes to the conclusion that after all, all is futility. And then, he pines on his own social relations and tidings of state affairs — they are now all severed from him. What can he do about them? Nothing now; so, let them be of their own accord.

(241) The second year of Dali (大历), the name of the reign of Dai-*zong* of Tang, was 767.

(242) In Kuizhou (夔州), called Fengjie *xian* (奉节县), Sichuan Province today, there was the official residence of the county governor or sheriff (刺史), in whom was invested the highest authority in civil as well as military affairs of the region. Yuanchi (元持) was the deputy governor (别驾).

(243) The fifth year of Kaiyuan during Xuan-*zong*'s reign was 717, when our poet was a child of six years only. In the prose introduction to the poem of some current texts, we have 开元三载, the character 三 of which is a misprint. In the third year of Kaiyuan, the poet was only four years old, too small a child to be a spectator of the dance. Du Fu was born in 712, the last year of Rui-*zong*'s (睿宗) reign and a year before Xuan-*zong* ascended his throne; in the fifth year of Kaiyuan, 717, he was six years old, or eight years old according to the lunar calendar of Xia (夏历) and calculated in the customary Chinese way.

(244) The two troupes of *danseuses* Yichun (宜春) and Liyuan (梨园) were instituted within the enclosure of the court walls. There were troupes of *danseuses* and men-dancers formed outside the court walls. The number of dancers male and female totalled several hundreds; to say, as in line 15 of Du Fu's original poem, that there were "eight thousand waiting maids of

the late emperor," is an exaggeration.

(245) Sage-artistic and Holy-militant Emperor (圣文神武皇帝) was a title of Xuan-*zong* offered to him for adulation by his courtiers in the 27th year of his reign Kai-yuan.

(246) Zhang Xu (张旭), noted for his wild *cao* (狂草) mode of calligraphy, flourished during the Kaiyuan and Tianbao years (713–755) of Xuan-*zong*'s reign. Li Bai's poetry, Pei Min's (裴旻) sword dance and Zhang Xu's *cao* calligraphy were known as the Three Supremacies (三绝) of the time. Zhang said his art pranced forward by leaps and bounds after his having enjoyed the spectacle of Gongsun's sword dance.

(247) According to legendary lore, Yi (羿) the great archer and *Di* Yao's (帝尧) courtier shot down nine out of the ten suns for their scorching and withering the green vegetation, thus saving all plant life and the human world.

(248) For fifty years, from the fifth year of Kaiyuan (开元五年，717) to the second year of Dali (大历二年，767), the rebellion of An Lushan and Shi Siming had almost overthrown the Li house and its Tang Dynasty.

(249) Li, the Twelfth Lady of Linying (临颖第十二娘), is the "one bright star still sparkling." She performed her sword dance in November 767 (大历二年十月).

(250) Xuan-*zong*, the emperor our poet has in mind here, died in 762 and was buried the next year on Jinsu-*shan* (金粟山), Golden Millet Mount, in Pucheng *xian* (蒲城县), Shaanxi Province today. The trees planted before his mausoleum five years ago have grown tall when this poem is written.

(251) "The stone-walled town" alludes to Baidi Town (白帝城), wherefrom the Linying Lady comes; it is in the vicinity of the Qutang Gorge (瞿塘峡) that "The grasses are bare."

(252) Watching the excellent sword dance with high spirits for having seen the acme of graceful dancing of Lady Gongsun during the early Kaiyuan years still vibrantly alive in her disciple's performance, the poet yet pines with sad thoughts on the calamitous happenings to Emperor Xuan-*zong*, the ruling house and the people at large. He lingers on what has just passed and refrains from stepping forth into reality and reminiscent miseries.

(253) The three-storied Yueyang Tower (岳阳楼) is a structure over the western gate of Yueyang's city wall overlooking the Dongting Lake (洞庭湖). It was built by the poet Zhang Yue (张说，667–730) of Tang when he was demoted from his original high post as the Imperial Secretary (中书令), Duke of Yan (燕国公), in the central government and banished to Yueyang

as its governor.

(254) Dongting Lake was anciently known as the Xiang Stream (湘水). In the *Classic of Streams* (《水经注》), the waters of Dongting Lake are described to be over 500 *li* in girth and the sun and moon seem to rise from and fall into it.

(255) It is said that "In the third year of the Dali Period (大历三年，768) of Dai-*zong*'s (代宗) reign, Guo Ziyi (郭子仪) commanding an army 50,000 strong stationed at Fengtian (奉天) to guard against Tubo (吐蕃), and his generals Bai Yuanguang (白元光) and Li Baoyu (李抱玉) led divisions to attack the foe."

(256) Zhuge Liang, or Kong Ming (诸葛亮，孔明，181–234), a native of the Langya (琅琊) County of Lu (鲁), was the renowned statesman and strategist of Shu-Han during the Three Kingdoms Period. He was thrice visited by Liu Bei (刘备，161–223) in his thatched cottage on the Longzhong Hills (隆中山), when he was a youthful anchorite only twenty-seven years old farming in Deng *xian* (邓县), at present Xiangyang (襄阳) *xian* of Hubei Province (湖北省), before he could be met with to consult on matters of the general political situation of the time. When Cao Pi (曹丕，187–226), the son of Cao Cao (曹操，155–220), usurped the Han throne in 220 as Wen-*di* of Wei (魏文帝), Zhuge counselled Liu Bei to declare himself the legitimate successor to the Han throne and was made by Liu his chancellor in 221. After the decease of Liu Bei, he upheld with might the prince Liu Shan (刘禅，207–271) in his weak reign till his own untimely death.

By the side of Liu Bei's temple in the western part of Chengdu, the chief city of Sichuan Province today, is located the Memorial Hall of Zhuge Liang, in the front of which is a giant cedar said to be planted by the Chancellor himself. The western portion of Chengdu was the ancient Town of Brocade-Gowned Officials (锦官城). According to *The Life of Zhuge Liang* (《诸葛亮传》) in Chen Shou's (陈寿) *Chronicle of the Three Kingdoms* (《三国志》), the Chancellor led in person the state's dispatch of troops via Xiegu (斜谷), to occupy Wugong (武功) and Fifty-Feet Plain (五丈原) to face in opposition to Sima Yi (司马懿), the Wei (魏) general of Cao Cao at Weinan (渭南). He remained at his post as commander for more than three months, till his own death in the camps.

(257) The original "空" when translated literally is "in vain".

(258) This poem was written by Du Fu as a captive in Chang'an, the capital of Tang, after it was occupied by the rebellious Hu (胡) satrap, An

Lushan's troops as the result of the smashing defeat of the imperial army commanded by the chancellor Fang Guan (房琯) at Chentao Incline (陈陶斜) and Qingban (青板), with tens of thousands of casualties.

(259) Gourd shell was used for holding foodstuff and tea, and mug for wine.

(260) In the sixth moon of the fifteenth year of the Tianbao Period (天宝十五年, 756) of Xuan-*zong*'s reign, the rebellion broke out that was to last for more than seven years. In the seventh moon, our poet left his family at the village Qiang (羌村) of Fuzhou (鄜州) for Lingwu (灵武), where the prince royal had ascended the throne as Su-*zong* (肃宗). He was captured on the way by the rebel forces and taken back to Chang'an. The next spring he composed his *Spring Prospects* (《春望》).

(261) The literal meaning of this line in the original is "(I) sit sadly (and) write (with my hand) in the air (strokes of the characters) '咄咄怪事' ('Huh, huh, what a strange thing!')." This is an allusion to an anecdote in the book *The World's Tales and Anecdotes Newly Related* (《世说新语》) written by Liu Yiqing (刘义庆) in the Song Dynasty of Liu (刘宋, 420–479): Yin Hao (殷浩), when he was relieved of his office, sat alone and wrote in the air the four characters "咄咄怪事" (Huh, huh, what an oddity!) the whole day.

(262) In the first moon of the Yongtai Period (永泰元年, 765) of Dai-*zong*'s reign, Du Fu resigned from his office under Yan Wu (严武, 726–765). In the fourth moon, Yan died. In the fifth, Du Fu left his thatched cot in Chengdu with his family to sail eastwards. When his ship passed Yuzhou (渝州), called Chongqing today, and Zhongzhou (忠州), now called Zhong *xian* (忠县), he wrote this octave. He was then fifty-two years old.

(263) In this line, the poet means to say that he is noted not merely as a man of letters, but also as a figure notable in political affairs. In the next line, he insinuates that he was forced to resign his office out of displeasure. And in the last two lines, he pictures himself in irony as a man badly belittled.

(264) Li Bai is meant here, whose nickname "the exiled faery" (谪仙) was given him by He Zhizhang (贺知章), a contemporary poet, on reading his poetry. Li and Du Fu, his good friend, were the two greatest poets of the illustrious Tang Dynasty. Han Yu, the writer of this poem, lived some three generations later than Li and Du and was a great poet as well as a master of prose, an eminent scholar and a fearless political figure.

(265) King Xuan of Zhou (周宣王, 827–781 BC) is renowned in Chinese history for his revival of that dynasty from its enfeebled state during the reigns previous to his, to the state of its glorious beginning in the times

of King Wu (武王) and King Cheng (成王). Thus, King Yi (夷王), his grandfather, crowned in 885 BC, broiled his vassal Duke Ai of Qi (齐哀公) in a big bronze tripodal two-eared sacrificial vessel. And King Li (厉王), his father, crowned in 877 BC, when threatened by an uprising of his subjects in 841 BC, fled from his capital to Zhi (彘) and afterwards died there. These two monarchs of Zhou are noted for their violence and cruelty, as well as King Xuan's son, King You (幽王), who was killed by foreign invaders in 771 BC. Xuan-*wang* was a ruler quite different from them. Two years after he ascended his throne, he dispatched large-scale campaigns against the Western Rong tribes (西戎) in the northwest and two years later against the Yan-yun tribes (严允) in the north, which in the times of Qin and Han (秦, 汉) were the Xiong-nu tribes (the Huns, 匈奴). In 823–822 BC, he ordered marches against the Jing-man, Huai-yi and Xu-rong tribes (荆蛮, 淮夷, 徐戎) in the south and the southeast, and conquered them all. The Stone Drums were expressly fabricated to commemorate the occasion of his triumph when a royal hunting expedition was undertaken to celebrate it, according to the poet and many others. These Drums are over three feet in diameter, the script being carved in large *zhuan* (大篆), the type of old calligraphy created by Shi Zhou (史籀), Grand Curator of History and Astronomy (太史) of Xuan-*wang*. Some other scholars attribute the date of these monuments earlier to the reign of King Cheng. Still others think they were executed as late as in the Qin Dynasty. Ouyang Xiu (欧阳修), a great scholar, historian, poet, prose master and political figure in the middle of the Song Dynasty, states in his *Antique Remains* (《集古录》) in the latter half of the 11th century that he had seen only 465 characters of these Drums. The earliest extant rubbing now in the collection of old, rare books in the Tianyi-*ge* (天一阁) Library in Zhejiang Province has only 462 characters. Poems and *fu* on the same subject were written by Wei Yingwu (韦应物), early Tang poet, Su Shi (苏轼), great Song poet, prose master, calligrapher, painter and political figure, and others besides this piece by Han Yu. In short, apart from the political importance of the historical record, the type of large *zhuan* calligraphy of the notation is unique by itself, as distinguished from the small *zhuan* (小篆), originated with Li Si (李斯).

(266) Qiyang (岐阳), the town in the south of the Qi Mountains, is at present Qi-*shan xian* (岐山县), Shaanxi (陕西).

(267) *Li shu* (隶书) is a type of calligraphy posterior to small *zhuan* and prior to *zhen shu* (真书). It was devised by Cheng Miao (程邈) in the Qin

Dynasty. *Ke* (蝌) is an abbreviation of *kedou* (蝌蚪), an early type of Zhou calligraphy resembling the tadpole.

(268) The water-dragon (蛟) is actually a nonentity supposed in folklore to be the cause of flood gushing forth from mountains. The *ling-tuo* (灵鼍) was said to be a crawling amphibian of the crocodile family with four claws, over twenty feet in length and fearful in its barkings and growlings. It was a peculiar wild brute of some of China's rivers and lakes. Its skin could be used for making big drums. It was also called the *tuo*-dragon or hog-dragon. The images in these five lines are descriptive of the calligraphic virtuosity of the large *zhuan* characters on the rubbing.

(269) Poems and ballads were collected extensively from the countryside as well as from the court and the ancestral temple of the royal family by a special organ of the government during the earlier reigns of Zhou. The inscription of the Stone Drums was neglected by the "ribald scholars" in their collection of *ya* poems, which were short lyrics only, the poet says here. It was Confucius who made the selection of the 305 pieces from the mass, that has formed *The Classic of Poetry* (*Shi Jing*《诗经》) — The *Book of Odes*, the rest having been lost during the centuries. The two *ya*, great and small ones (大雅，小雅), are poems "written by courtiers about court affairs with the intent of exhortation, the feelings of loyalty and filial piety and the compassion relevant to these, signifying what is good and disapproving the ill, earnestly related and clearly expressed so as to make the hearer deeply touched."

(270) In his travels through various states late in the Spring and Autumn Period (春秋，770–477 BC) of Zhou to find a master worthy of himself, Confucius did not go far westward to enter Qin (秦), perhaps more for the reason that Qin was "a state of tiger and wolf" than that it was too far west. The next statement is figurative rather than literal, for he had nothing to do with picking departing souls for raising them to be stars. In ancient times, people of great eminence were believed to be transformed into stars when they died. The line means to say that even Confucius was not vigilant of a thousand and one things: he might miss one or two inadvertantly. Xihe (羲和) was the legendary driver of the Sun chariot and Ehuang (娥皇) was the queen of Emperor Shun (帝舜) of Yu (虞), daughter of Emperor Yao (帝尧) of Tang (唐).

(271) Han Yu was ordained a doctor of the Imperial College (大学) to lecture on literature by the authorities concerned in the first year of Emperor Xian-zong's (宪宗) new reign named Yuanhe (元和，806).

(272)   The Drums, first verified in Tang at the time of the poet after they had been long forgotten, were located in the wilds of Chencang (陈仓), a *xian* now known as Baoji (宝鸡), Shaanxi, which was in the right (western) vicinity of the capital Chang'an, as one looked southerly.

(273)   The bronze tripodal two-eared vessel *ding* (鼎), symbol of political sovereignty, placed in the ruler's ancestral temple, of the ducal state Song (宋), in its capital South Gao (南郜) is implied to be a war spoil when that city was captured, according to the *Spring and Autumn Annals* (《春秋》). This particular trophy, then, has taken on a general connotation here, and therefore means simply any such trophy in the Imperial Ancestral Temple of Li Tang (李唐). The importance of this vessel could be traced back to the nine *ding* cast by King Yu of Xia (夏禹), the great benefactor of the indigenous Chinese race and the first of the Three Kindly Kings (三王), who saved the people from extinction by conducting the deluge to the sea and set the lunar calendar now still in partial use, to name two of his great deeds.

(274)   Evidently, an exhibition of the classics, presumably Confucian in substance, brushed on scrolls during Han, Wei, Jin and the Six Dynasties (汉，魏，晋，六朝), was held sometime before this poem was composed, at the shire town Hongdu newly founded (洪都新府) during early Tang. The city is today known as Nanchang (南昌) of Jiangxi Province. Hongdu was made famous by the great early Tang poet Wang Buo (王勃) in his splendid *fu* (赋), *Proem to the Teng-wang Pavilion* (《滕王阁序》).

(275)   Wang Xizhi (王羲之), the great calligrapher of Jin (晋), whose *li, cao* and *xing* types of *shu* (隶，草，行书) are matchless throughout the ages, was said to be fond of watching white geese. Once he came upon a flock of them and offered to buy them from a Shanyin taoist priest (山阴道士). He was asked by their owner to brush on some sheets of paper the *Dao-de Classic* (《道德经》) of Lao-*zi* (老子，not *Huangting Classic*, 《黄庭经》, also written by Lao-*zi*, mistakenly attributed by the great poet Li Bai to be brushed by Wang Xizhi for winning him the geese) and the geese were gladly presented to him in exchange.

(276)   Confucius and Mencius. Their original names in Chinese are Kong Qiu (孔丘) and Meng Ke (孟轲).

(277)   The tone of this quatrain in the original is one of desolation and time's mutability. The Cinnabar Bird Bridge (朱雀桥) was built during the Xiankang year (咸康，335–342) in the reign of Cheng-*di* (成帝，325–343) of East Jin (东晋，317–420) as a buoyant bridge on the Qinhuai River

(秦淮河). The site of the Black Coat Lane (乌衣巷) is in the south of the Qinhuai River at Nanjing (南京), Jiangsu Province. The locality had served during the Three Kingdoms Period (220–280) as the barracks of the Black-Coated (Doublet) Battalion of the state Wu, hence the lane's name. Wang Dao (王导) and Xie An (谢安) were premiers of East Jin; their families were notable during the Six Dynasties and so were their residences. They have passed away long ago and nobodies have taken their places now in these premises. The third and fouth lines could be rendered thus:

> The swallows 'fore the former notable houses
> Now fly into the common folks' homestalls.

(278) The ancient site of the Stone-Walled City (石头城) is around the Qing-liang Hills (清凉山) of Nanjing today. During the Warring States Period (战国，476–221 BC), it was the city Jinling (金陵) of the state Chu (楚). During the Three Kingdoms Period, Sun Quan (孙权), king of the state Wu, rebuilt the city and called it the Stone-Walled City. "The tides" in the second line mean those of the Yangtze River which beat the desolate old city and lonelily ebb again and again. Huai Stream means the Qinhuai River (秦淮河), which flowed past the city, very prosperous during the Six Dynasties "the old time," and still flows as of old. As the beams of the old-time moon cross the low parapet to shine on the west, the scene appears very desolate indeed.

(279) Liu Zongyuan (773–819), whose courtesy name is Zihou (子厚), was a native of Hedong (河东), at present Yongji *xian* (永济县) of Shanxi Province. He passed the imperial examination of *jinshi* (进士), the candidate qualified for being elected to high officialdom during De-*zong*'s (德宗) Zhenyuan years (贞元，785–805). During the reign of Shun-*zong* (顺宗), he and his friend and fellow scholar of the examination Liu Yuxi (刘禹锡) together with Wang Pi (王伾), took part in Wang Shuwen's (王叔文) Reform Movement group against corruption, tax extortion of the subjects and compulsory contributions from local officials, oppression in general and the eunuchs cabal. The eunuchs plotted a coup d'état forcing the emperor to be dethroned and inherit his sway to the imperial prince. Wang Shuwen was executed. Liu Zongyuan was degraded in his banishment to Yongzhou (永州) as a country official and later therefrom to Liuzhou (柳州). When he was exiled to his second post, he heard Liu Yuxi was exiled to Bozhou (播州), which is Zunyi (遵义) of Guizhou Province (贵州省) today. The latter town was a most miserable spot for human habitation. Besides, Liu Yuxi had an aged mother in the capital, who could not go to

stay at such an impossible border town. For his friend's sake, Liu Zongyuan implored to go himself to Bozhou and let Liu Yuxi go to Liuzhou instead. Fortunately, some influtial court officials begged for mercy and succeeded to have Liu Yuxi exiled to Lianzhou (连州). Our poet's nobility of character as shown in this affair alone has ranked him an illustrious figure in China's literary history. His prose writings have made him a celebrated co-master of the "Old Prose School" (古文派) with Han Yu (韩愈) of the Tang Dynasty and Ouyang Xiu (欧阳修) and Su Shi (苏轼) of the Song Dynasty. His prose pieces in recording his trips to various scenic spots round Yongzhou and Liuzhou are notable for their lucidity and scintillating picturesqueness. In his *Preface* to *Poems Written by the Fool's Runlet* (《愚溪诗序》), our poet says, "In the north of Guan Stream (灌水) there is a runlet flowing eastward into Xiao Stream (潇水). Someone said that a certain Ran (冉) family resided there; so the water was named the Ran Runlet (冉溪). Someone else said that the water could be used for dyeing; so it was once named the Dye Runlet (染溪). I have committed the grave offense with my folly and was exiled to the Xiao Stream Valley. I love the runlet. Following the currents for two or three *li*, I have found an excellent spot to make my dwelling. In ancient days, there was the Foolish Sire's Valley (愚公谷). Now I build my abode by the runlet and, for lack of a proper name to be given to the water, as my neighbours contend that I must change the old name for a new one, I call it the Fool's Runlet (愚溪). Above the Fool's Runlet, I have bought a hillock which I call the Fool's Hillock (愚丘) from which walking northeastward some sixty steps, I come to a spring which I have also acquired and named the Fool's Spring (愚泉). The spring has six mouths, all issuing from the flat land by the side of the hills and flowing together tortuously southward to form what I call the Fool's Creek (愚沟). Then I dug out and heaped up clay, studded with rocks, to excavate my Fool's Pond (愚池). Towards the east of the Pond, I have erected the Fool's Hall (愚堂), in the south of it the Fool's Arbour (愚亭) and in the middle of the water I have piled up the Fool's Ait (愚岛) with fair trees and quaint rockeries on it. All these are spotlighted picturesque gems of the landscape, but all bear the shame of folly for my sake."

(280) The poet draws in this poem his spiritual self-portrait in his exile thousands of *li* away from Chang'an (长安), the imperial city, to Yongzhou (永州) way down in the south.

(281) This is an excellent satirical poem with its thorns hidden under the obviously plain statements regarding the common knowledge about the

beauty of the third elder sister of the imperial concubine, the Queen of the State of Guo (虢国夫人), who was exclusively allowed by special permission of the Emperor himself to ride into the palace gate at early morn, which was strictly forbidden to the chief courtiers, even the chancellor himself, right before or after the period of formal court attendance. She was in Xuan-*zong*'s "supreme favour." Priding herself on her natural beauty, she declined to resort to cosmetics, rouge and eyebrow pencil for enhancing her looks. The promiscuous relations between the emperor and her were an open secret at the court and to the public, and her similar relations with her so-called cousin Yang Guozhong (see Note 152 of Du Fu's poem *The Lay of the Belles*) were also well-known at the court and to the populace, except perhaps the sole person, Xuan-*zong*.

Jiling Terrace was on the Li Mounts (骊山) for paying homage to the gods. The Li Mounts were where the Li Tribesmen (骊戎) had been inhabiting during the Spring and Autumn Period (春秋，770–477 BC) of the Zhou Dynasty (周朝，1046–256 BC). The Li Mounts are today in the southeast of Lintong *xian* (临潼县), connected with the Lantian Mounts (蓝田山) of Lantian *xian* (蓝田县), of Shaanxi Province.

(282) The Clear-and-Bright Feast (清明) of spring has been a religious festival in China from time immemorial. On this day in mid-spring, April 5th or 6th, people visit the burying places of their ancestors to do obeisance or pay homage and sweep the tombs. It is the 105th or 106th day from the winter solstice (冬至).

(283) According to *The Book of Sovereignty Homage* of the *Han Chronicle* (《汉书·郊祀志》), the wizards say, in the time of the Luteous Emperor (黄帝), Twelve Storeyed Houses were built in Five Walled Expanses (五城十二楼) to greet the faeries, called "Welcoming the Year" (迎年). Ying Shao's (应劭) note on this is: "In xuan-*pu* (玄圃) on the Kunlun Mountains (昆仑山), the Twelve Storeyed Houses in the Five Walled Expanses are where the faeries permanently reside."

(284) A gifted poet of late Tang, Wen Tingyun's name is often accompanied by Li Shangyin, who however excels in imaginative quality. In the collection *Among the Flowers* (《花间集》), Wen is the foremost composer of *ci* (词), an outgrowth of *shi* (诗) rising during middle Tang, characterized by being sung and tuned with musical instruments. He was a frequent visitor to houses of singing girls and his life career was unhappy as a result of offending the powerful. His style is sometimes decorative. The title means "sad songs played on the ancient harp adorned with gems." According to

The World's Records (《世本》), said to be compiled by chroniclers during the Warring States (战国，403–221 BC), "the harp was first made by Bao Xi (庖牺), our earliest ancestor, with fifty strings and placed on a wooden frame when being plucked. The Luteous Emperor (黄帝，2694–2597 BC) made it an intrument of twenty-five strings."

(285)　The Gladdening Uplands were an elevated plain forming the spacious southern precinct of Chang'an, the capital of the Tang Dynasty. They were a pleasurable park region overlooking the splendid, populous part of the imperial city.

(286)　During the Zhou Dynasty (周朝，1046–256 BC), Ba (巴) was a feudal state paying homage to the king of Zhou, the Son of Heaven. Qin (秦，221–206 BC) annexed it and made it a county of its empire. At the end of East Han (东汉，25–220), two more counties were instituted from it by the count palatine of Yizhou (益州牧) Liu Zhang (刘璋), named East Ba and West Ba, called in all the Three Ba (三巴). The Tang Dynasty (唐朝，618–907) blotted the two later names and gave them new ones. North Zhou (北周，557–581) of the North Dynasty (北朝，386–581) began to call the capital of old Ba *xian* (巴县). The Three Ba regions of ancient Shu (蜀), the present Sichuan Province, are a mountainous district. This poem was written by Li Shangyin to his wife Lady Li-Wang during his visit to the Ba-Shu regions in the autumn of the second year of the Dazhong period (大中三年，849) in Xuan-*zong*'s (唐宣宗) reign of the Tang Dynasty. Its tortuous circumstances and the poet's relevant feelings are of notable nostalgic beauty. When he was writing these lines, it was raining in the hilly Ba-Shu district outside of his house; he was not sure when he would sit with her below the western window of their home, clipping the candle wick to make the flame shine brighter, and talk to her of his feelings for her this night.

(287)　Chang'e (嫦娥) of exquisite beauty, originally called Heng'e (姮娥), was the queen of Hou Yi (后羿), the king of Dynasty Xia's (夏朝，2070–1600 BC) tributary state Youqiong (有穷). Yi obtained the immortal herb from the fairy lady West Wang Mother (西王母). Heng'e stole the immortal herb of her husband, ate it and fled to the moon. She had to reside there alone through eternity. Hou Yi, a great archer, was reputed in legendary lore to have shot down nine out of ten suns in his time. He set up a dictatorship, ruled Xia for 49 years till he was killed by his own henchman Han Zhuo (寒浞).

(288)　The Cold Repast (寒食) was a feast held for three days from the 105th day to the 107th after the previous year's winter solstice. It usually commenced on the 4th or 5th of April, or the previous day to the Clear-and-Bright Feast (清明) in the third moon of the lunar year. The feast has been observed for centuries to memorize Jie Tui (介推), a faithful follower of Duke Wen of State Jin (晋文公) in the Spring and Autumn Period, who accompanied the young prince in his flee to the state Qi (齐) but was forgotten to be rewarded when the prince came back to be installed as the head of the state. In anger, Jie Tui left the court and retired to Mount Mian (绵山) as a recluse with his old mother. The young duke, soon aware of Jie's absence, sensed his own fault and dispatched men to induce Jie back to court to compensate him, but the messengers failed to locate Jie. An order was given to burn the weeds on the mount with the hope that the spreading wild fire would drive Jie down. In wrath at the young Duke's ingratitude, Jie clasped a tree trunk and was found burnt to death. The remorseful prince did penance to Jie Tui in sackcloth and ashes, ordered that thereafter no brushwood should be cut from Mount Mian and a feast of three days should be set up as Cold Repast (寒食), during which no fire should be lit to cook food. The feast is still partially observed today, for during the occasion people eat cold green dumplings stuffed with mashed red beans, though the practice of prohibiting fire to cook food has long been ignored out of memory. Most people are wholly ignorant of the origin why they eat cold stuffed dumplings on certain days in the spring at present.